The **Vampire** and The **Vegan**

Book I: Food

Merlene Alicia Vassall

First Edition

Mount Rainier, MD

The Vampire and The Vegan
Book I: Food by Merlene Alicia Vassall

Technical Assistance & Support Consultants
P.O. Box 69
Mount Rainier, MD 20712-2111 U.S.A.
http://www.technicalassistance.com
http://www.vampireandvegan.com

ISBN-13: 978-0-615-40420-2

Cover art by Kevin Richardson, Kebo Designs, LLC
Photo by Jorge Mera

Printed in the United States of America

Library of Congress Control Number: 2010938990

Acknowledgments

I would like to thank the following individuals and organizations that contributed their time, talent, knowledge, constructive criticism, support, and encouragement to the development and promotion of this novel:

Afrika Afeni Mills ✦ Anne Powell ✦ Carmen Gillmore Scott Carmen Robles-Inman ✦ Charles A. Sessoms ✦ Clyde McElvene David Banks ✦ David Herring ✦ Deborah Dickson Jones Eric Priest ✦ Eric Walker ✦ Fathom Creative ✦ Grace Kelly Hasan Ashshaheed ✦ Hurston/Wright Foundation Ibrahim Gassama ✦ Imani Afryka ✦ Jaiya John Janet Silverthorne ✦ Joan Lee ✦ John Vassall ✦ Jonathan Balcolme Jorge Mera ✦ Kaifa Anderson-Hall ✦ Kebo Designs Kenneth Carroll ✦ Kevin Richardson ✦ Kisha Kantasingh Mangierlett Garris ✦ Martha Castaneda ✦ Marya McQuirter Mat Johnson ✦ Minnedore Green ✦ Miriam Cotton ✦ Morgan Lowe National Novel Writing Month ✦ Nimat Jones Nona Mitchell-Richardson ✦ Olive Allen ✦ Patricia Lee Saundra Woods ✦ Saurabh Dalal ✦ Sherry Essig Stephanie Redcross ✦ Steven Noel ✦ Tracye McQuirter Twiggy ✦ Two-Face ✦ Two-Face, Jr. ✦ Vegan Mainstream Vegetarian Society of DC ✦ Vernon Ware ✦ Zakia Shabazz

You're the best!

Merlene

I said in mine heart concerning the estate of the sons of men, that God might manifest them, and that they might see that they themselves are beasts.

For that which befalleth the sons of men befalleth beasts; even one thing befalleth them: as the one dieth, so dieth the other; yea, they have all one breath; so that a man hath no preeminence above a beast; for all is vanity.

All go unto one place; all are of the dust, and all turn to dust again.

— Ecclesiastes 3:18-20

Chapter 1

I walked into Christopher's Seafood Restaurant, and before the *maître d'* could seat me, I had already spotted my next meal. Tall, handsome, and well-dressed, he appeared to be in his thirties. His skin was a rich caramel color, and his shoulder-length dreadlocks were each exactly the same thickness and length. His short goatee was also painstakingly groomed. I smiled as the word "dapper" came to mind. I guess "metrosexual" is the more modern term.

Most women would have probably focused on the muscularity of his arms and chest – clearly visible through his lavender silk shirt – or his firm, round buttocks for that matter, but what allured me was his choice of entree: lobster.

I watched intently as he carefully selected his prey from the large fish tank that had been situated just inside the entrance to the restaurant. This was an obvious attempt to entice those with a taste for freshly killed sea animals. He pointed out the largest lobster and watched lustfully as the chef's assistant removed the tired and bewildered animal from the cloudy, gray water. His claws had been restrained with two thick rubber bands, but this was unnecessary. There was no way for him to escape, nowhere for him to go, and he was too confused and exhausted to fight any longer. In a few minutes, he would experience the searing pain of being boiled alive.

The dapper man returned to his table and his date, an attractive young woman of no consequence. I knew that he would be leaving with me. I waited impatiently to be seated, my hunger piqued now that dinner was so imminent.

This was my first time at this particular restaurant, but it was frequently mentioned in the "Style" section of *The Washington Post* as one of the hot gathering spots for young professionals who thought themselves to be destined for greatness. The decor was pleasant enough. The walls were painted a deep green with intricate mahogany wainscoting and woodwork surrounding the many floor-to-ceiling windows facing out onto the Potomac River. The tiny, flickering flames of the candles on the tables mirrored the stars outside. But the odor of seafood mixed uneasily with the sweet scent of rum buns for which the restaurant was apparently known.

"Good evening," the young woman serving as *maitre d'* finally greeted me. "How many in your party?"

"Just one."

"Would you like a table by the window?"

"No. A seat at the end of the bar."

As I followed her the short distance, I felt a deep emptiness in my gut. My body was aching for nourishment, and the sensation was almost unbearable. It was as if my insides were caving in, and I was even getting a little lightheaded. Yet my visible demeanor never changed. No one who looked at me could see even a hint of the intense hunger that I was experiencing.

Gracefully, I seated myself on the bar stool, crossing my legs to reveal their sensuous contours accented by black silk stockings and stiletto heels. The hem of my dress rode up to mid thigh. From the vantage point of the bar, I would be able to see and be seen by my prey.

I wouldn't have much longer to wait. Despite his banter with his date, it was clear that my target had noticed me, and he was unable to stop glancing in my direction.

He was momentarily distracted as the waiter brought the dead crustacean to his table, along with a shrimp entree for the young woman. Once the food arrived, the couple's conversation ceased. I watched as the man used a nutcracker to break the animal's claw, and a fork to pull out the soft tissue within. He dipped the flesh into a small bowl of melted butter, put it into his mouth, and slowly chewed, savoring the flavor in a manner that was almost erotic.

I caught his eye and deliberately held his gaze for a moment too long. Then I bent over to brush an imaginary speck from the top of my shoe. This offered him a glimpse of cleavage peeking out over the plunging neckline of the lipstick-red dress that I had chosen for tonight's hunt. He smiled at me. I stared into his eyes and enthralled him.

He was now doomed, like a hungry fish drawn to a fisherman's bait, unaware that within the tasty morsel lies a jagged hook about to tear into his flesh. The one seeking a meal would become a meal himself. I could hardly wait.

I continued to watch my prey enjoy his meal for a while longer. It would be his last, and I wanted him to finish it. But he was a slow eater, and I could see that his date was trying to make conversation. I was starving!

"Good evening." The bartender interrupted my thoughts, and I turned my head to look at him. He was young and appeared to be of Italian or Middle Eastern descent. He had straight, jet black hair and olive skin and was clad in the typical bartender uniform of a white dress shirt and black pants. "What will you be drinking this evening?"

I smiled to myself. "A Bloody Mary."

"Unusual choice. Mixes good nutrition with poison." He waited for a reply that never came. "Would you like to see a menu?"

"No. Just the drink. Where are the restrooms?"

"Back there, behind that wall," the bartender gestured and smiled at me. I guess I hadn't made my disinterest clear enough. "Don't worry," he said. "I'll be sure to save your seat for you."

"I never worry," I said coldly and turned away from him.

I figured that my prey had had enough time to complete most of his meal, so I stood up and looked at him again. Predictably, he was still staring at me even as his date continued to chatter. Without uttering a word, I commanded him to follow me and walked slowly across the room. My stomach was beginning to contract, but I remained outwardly calm.

He was right behind me by the time I reached the wall that separated the restrooms from the main dining area. Even before I turned around, I knew he was there. As he came closer to me, the air changed. It became tangible and electric.

When we were both out of view of his date, he said, "Hey, pretty lady. Did you ask me to follow you, or was I imagining things?"

"I sent the message, and you received it. Get rid of your date, and take me to your place."

"What? Right now? Are you serious?"

"Very."

"Damn!" he said with a combination of both shock and awe. He looked me up and down in such a lustful manner that I would have been offended – if only I cared what humans thought of me. "Just give me a few minutes. I'll be right with you."

I returned to the bar, and he went to his table. Standing over his date, he whispered in her ear. I tuned out the other sounds in the restaurant and focused on their conversation.

"We have to leave," he said to her in a hushed voice.

"Why? What happened?"

"When I was in the bathroom, I got a call from Derrick. You know he's always getting himself into something. I gotta go and bail him out of some mess."

"Really. What exactly is his problem?"

"You know. Something with some girl. I can tell you about it later."

"You must really think I'm stupid, Tony."

"Here we go again! What are you talking about, *Lisa?*" He sat down on the edge of his seat, steeling himself for the argument.

"Do you think I didn't see you eyeballing that woman at the bar and meeting up with her in front of the bathrooms?" Her voice was beginning to rise. "I couldn't tell which was making you drool more, your lobster or her."

Tony glanced at me. "Oh please! Don't be ridiculous. I don't even know her."

"And that's what makes it all the more exciting! I remember how you were when we first met, three whole months ago! You have the attention span of a two year old."

"Things may not be as hot as they were, but whose fault is that? Anyway, I don't have time for this argument right now. I'm putting you in a cab, and we can talk later."

"I can manage to get myself home – without your assistance. This is it. Don't bother to call me again. I hope she's worth it."

Lisa opened her purse, threw some cash on the table, and hurried out of the restaurant.

Tony signaled to the waiter to bring the check. After he paid the bill, he came over to me at the bar. He was visibly upset, but he pulled himself together. Hunger was gnawing at my insides, but my appearance was relaxed.

"All right now, pretty lady. I did what you asked and got rid of her, even though I think that she was really into me. I hope you're ready to make it worth my while."

"I will be, as soon as you pay for my drink."

He frowned but placed a $10 bill on the bar for the Bloody Mary that I had not even touched.

"What's your name?" he asked as we walked out of the restaurant.

I was tempted to say "Mary" but figured that the irony would be lost on him, so I said, "Vanessa," which is not my name.

"I'm very pleased to make your acquaintance, Vanessa. I'm Tony."

I did not reply.

"My car's right across the street ... the silver, convertible Porsche there. It's a great car for driving with the top down on hot summer nights."

As we crossed the street, he unlocked the doors remotely with his key fob. I walked around to the passenger side and let myself in. Once he was comfortable in the leather seat, he retracted the roof and turned on the sound system, loud. We drove through the streets with his obnoxious rap music blasting a monotonous beat and spewing out lurid lyrics, and I knew I would enjoy ending his life.

After about fifteen minutes, while we were stopped at a light, he grabbed my chin and kissed me roughly on the lips, catching me by surprise. I guess he thought he was being sexy. I was furious but said nothing.

Another twenty minutes passed, and we parked behind a tall condominium building in the Chevy Chase area. As we entered, the contrast between the warm air outdoors and the cold air inside was harsh. Soon, we were at the door of his sixth floor apartment. I paused, waiting for an invitation to enter his home. I didn't actually need one, but this was a courtesy that I liked to maintain. Along with sexually arousing prey to release endorphin, it was a part of the humane slaughter tradition.

"Come on in."

Looking at his apartment, not to mention his car, it was clear that Tony prided himself in being a stylish lover above all else. The living room was furnished completely in black and white. Two black leather sofas flanked a white Mongolian fur rug, which lay in front of a marble fireplace. The walls were painted white, and black drapes pooled on the floor in front of the windows. The tables and lamps were made of glass, chrome, and more black leather. A mammoth television set was across from the fireplace. White candles and a few small sculptures had been placed throughout the room. It was neat, clean, colorless, and deadly cold.

I walked into the center of the room, took off my shoes, and stood on the rug in front of the empty fireplace. Then I turned to look at him.

Still standing by the door, Tony removed his shoes, took off his socks, and put one neatly in each shoe. He then placed the shoes side by side by the front door. Next, he turned on the television set with a remote that had been on an end table. An adult movie began, but the sound was just barely audible. An anonymous man and two Plasticine women were engaged in sexual acrobatics. Was this supposed to excite me?

It seemed that Tony had a routine that he was hell-bent on following. In silence, he retrieved a box of matches from the mantel and lit a musky incense stick that was already halfway burned. I remained standing. He turned on some soft jazz. He went to another room and returned with a bottle of wine and two glasses. As he placed them on the end table, I finally sat down on one of the sofas and watched him fill each glass halfway with white wine.

"I'll be right back," he said. "Don't go anywhere."

He left the room, *again,* and I decided to give him five more minutes, at best. I was famished and had lost patience long ago. I heard a toilet flush and the sounds of him brushing his teeth. I shook my head. Unbelievable!

Finally, Tony came back into the living room. Again, I stood in the middle of the rug, and he walked over to me. I began unbuttoning his shirt. The silk and mother-of-pearl buttons were smooth and cold against my fingers. I unbuckled his snake skin belt. As soon as I unfastened his pants, they fell to the floor. He had on black silk boxers, of course.

I placed my hands on his upper arms to keep him still and basked in the energy he radiated, moving my face slowly across and down his neck, shoulders, chest, abdomen, and groin. It almost overwhelmed my senses. This was going to be exquisite.

Tony pulled me up to a standing position and unzipped my dress to reveal my red lace teddy and lace-topped stockings. "Beautiful lady in red," he said softly.

I smiled at his cliched response. Men were so predictable and easily manipulated. I always wore red when I went out hunting because I knew that the color excited and agitated them. It seemed to elicit almost a reflex reaction, like the cape waved in front of a bull by the *matador* – Spanish for "killer."

Tony tried to kiss me on the mouth again, but I pulled away. Instead of kissing him, I picked up our clothing and tossed the pile onto one of the sofas. Tony seemed to be at a loss, confused by my behavior, so he remained almost motionless until I pulled him down onto the rug.

I paused to look at him for a moment. He was in an awkward position, not quite sitting, not quite kneeling.

"What are you waiting for? I'm dying to see what you have in mind. Enough with the suspense!"

"Lie flat on your back."

He obeyed, and I removed the decorative comb that had been holding my braided hair in a neat bun. It was sleek, simple, and made of smooth sterling silver. Two of the teeth were longer than the others, spaced about an inch apart. Very deliberately, I placed the comb on the rug, next to Tony's head.

As I straddled him, he eagerly cupped my breasts with his hands, which were surprisingly warm and soft. He ran them down my abdomen, but before he could go any further, I grabbed both of his wrists with my left hand and forcefully pushed them to the floor above his head. I held them there.

He smiled and exclaimed, "You're wicked, aren't you!"

"Very."

I picked up my comb and slowly dragged it down his left cheek, stopping at the side of his neck. At this point, he was still smiling, but his expression soon changed. I pressed the comb against him, and the two long teeth pierced his skin and sank into his carotid artery.

"What the hell are you doing?" he cried out in pain. I said nothing.

At first, he struggled to get up, but I held him fast, using my will more than my muscles to subdue him. He was a fool to think that he was stronger than I. And my aim had been precise. Soon a pool of blood was forming on the white fur rug.

"Be still," I commanded. His struggling ceased, but he continued to watch me in silent terror.

Once Tony was motionless, I noticed the jazz music playing and the sounds of the threesome on the life-sized television set, their exaggerated moans making a mockery of passion. But this was just a fleeting thought. My focus quickly returned to my meal.

Careful to avoid getting blood on me, I leaned over Tony's body and covered the wounds on his neck with my mouth. Blood coursed from his artery into my throat, and I could finally exploit the necromantic energy that he had accumulated during his lifetime of eating slaughtered animals.

Tony's offense may have been unwitting, but nevertheless, every action has a consequence. He probably didn't know that each animal's suffering and death at the hands of humans created mystical energy that permeated the animal's body. Each time Tony had eaten meat or any other substance derived from a brutalized creature, he had defiled himself, contaminated his own blood, and made himself enticing to those of us at the top of the food chain.

Now, he was fully charged, and I delighted in draining him. It invigorated me.

As I consumed Tony's blood, I witnessed the pathetic lives of the animals he had eaten passing before me like images on a movie screen, there for my entertainment. The energy from his last meal brought me to the greatest heights of ecstacy. I relished the terror and pain of the lobster who had been taken from his home, imprisoned, and boiled alive only an hour or two earlier. The creature had been stupid to let himself get caught! I reveled in its anguish – and the torment of several hundred animals whose flesh Tony had eaten over his lifetime. Their suffering flooded back more quickly and in less detail, but it was just as real and amusing to me.

This is what I had been waiting for, and what a feast! His tainted blood was warm and thick and a little bit bitter. It had a flavor and a power like no other substance, well worth the wait. Gulping it down, I became almost dizzy. I could feel myself getting stronger. I drank until I was cloyed, and then I drank a little more.

All in all, Tony was a very satisfying meal. And now he, too, was dead.

I wiped the blood off of my comb and returned it to my hair. *Funny,* I thought, *Tony's dead body is strangely beautiful and peaceful.*

I stood up, turned off the television, and put the air conditioning on an even lower setting, to keep Tony smelling fresh longer. Rifling through his music collection, I was surprised to find that he actually exhibited good taste.

What else might I discover? I walked around his apartment, absentmindedly touching and looking at his possessions: a set of golf clubs in a corner in the hallway, a wooden box of cigars on the desk in his den, a paddle emblazoned with the Greek letters of a fraternity on his kitchen wall. His refrigerator held little besides meat and animal products: chicken breasts, pork chops, steaks, eggs, cheese, and a lonely, half empty bottle of wine inside the door.

I returned to the den and took a cigar and matches from his desk. Still dressed in only a teddy and stockings, I sat on the leather couch in the living room with my toes in the fur rug. I liked the smell of a good cigar, so I lit it and set it down in a small dish on the end table.

What a wonderful night! Good food, good music – but all good things must come to an end, I thought.

I switched off the sound system and put my dress and shoes back on. Then I removed the car keys from Tony's pants and put them in my purse. Sated and in a much better mood, I turned around as I reached the door to take one last look at Tony. He was an excellent man!

I left the building and drove his car to Union Station. Leaving it in the parking lot, I took the escalator down two levels and exited the front of the huge edifice. Immediately, I caught a cab at the taxi stand and returned to my home to sleep peacefully.

Chapter 2

Three weeks had passed since I had made a meal of Tony, and I was hungry once again. Yet I was not at all in the mood to hunt. If I didn't have to eat, I would probably never leave home. I had grown increasingly loathe to mingle with humans – filthy vermin that leave a trail of destruction and disease wherever they go. In small numbers, they're good for labor and food, but that's the extent of their usefulness. The rest should be exterminated.

I could hardly believe that I had actually been one of them, once. But that was a long time ago, before Kwamena tasted me and turned me into a higher being.

I could still remember how confused I was right after the change, when Kwamena told me all about necromantic energy and the rules and traditions I should follow. He had explained my new powers to me – sensing people's thoughts, perceiving the nearly imperceptible, captivating a human with a mere look, subduing my prey with a simple word or two – yet it took me a few months of practice to perfect my techniques and develop a hunting strategy that suited me and always worked. Ironically, my first meal, a woman, led me to the answer: targeting men.

A few days after Kwamena had changed me, I grew hungry for necromantic energy. Unsure of how to capture my prey, I did what I was used to doing when I was restless. I put on a lacy black cocktail dress and headed to the piano lounge at The Waterfall, one of the most exclusive hotels in the city.

As I stood near the piano, cognac in hand, I basked in the energy of the men and women who brushed past me – teasing me, tempting me. I wanted to eat someone. Anyone would do, but I would have to get my prey alone, and I didn't know how to do that without arousing suspicion or leaving evidence.

In those days, I still had a fear of getting caught, not realizing how many homicides go unsolved every year, particularly once the victim's friends and family members were ruled out. At that time, I didn't know that it took two decades and ninety bodies before authorities caught the Green River Killer in Washington State, and it was three months before the Washington, DC snipers were caught – even though they shot more than a dozen people in public.

Back then, standing at the piano in that dark, smoky room, I thought I needed to come up with a clever plan to capture my prey and escape police detection. As I stood there thinking, too much time was passing, and eventually, the concierge noticed and approached me.

She was a young woman with big green eyes and straight, shoulder-length hair. Although she was wearing a teal hotel uniform, it was so stylish that I wouldn't have realized it wasn't an ordinary dress. Only her name tag gave it away.

"Excuse me, ma'am," Yvonne whispered to me. "I hate to do this, and I'm terribly embarrassed, but it's part of my job."

She put her hand on my elbow and gently steered me toward the end of the bar, where there were only a few other people.

"Recently, we've had some problems with... well, with women without, you know, the best of intentions... coming to our lounge and sort of looking for... men who might be interested in... spending some time and money on them. Please forgive me. I know that *couldn't* be you, but it's my job to ask if you are staying at this hotel or if you are meeting one of our guests here. Again, I'm sorry to have to ask you this."

I smiled at her discomfort and leaned in close to whisper my response. As I did so, the energy that she was emitting washed over me and made my entire body tingle. She was delectable! I was emboldened and decided to take a chance.

"What if I told you that I *don't* have the best of intentions," I said in a slow, steady voice. "In fact, my only intention right now is to find a monied man who is willing to share his wealth with me for a lifetime – or at least an evening."

"I... I... I appreciate your honesty." She leaned away from me and studied my face, obviously intrigued and looking for the right words to say. She moved in close to me again, her full lips nearly brushing against my ear. "Have you been successful at it? Are you making good money? Do men actually buy you expensive things?"

I put my hand on her shoulder and whispered my answer to her. "Would I be here if they didn't? And I only choose the tastiest men. I don't know why you're wasting your youth working for this hotel. You could be making a killing!"

"Really? You really think I could?"

"Of course!"

"I don't know... I see all these men here with so much money... Some of them are kind of handsome. It's just a crazy fantasy of mine."

"It doesn't have to be. You could be making top dollar for something that you'd do for free. But you need to know how to attract the right type of man and how to get him to open up his wallet. It's all in the technique. I can show you. I'd love to have a partner. So tell me, when do you get off?"

She glanced at her watch. "In about twenty minutes." She took a deep breath and held it for several seconds. Finally, she exhaled, and I knew I had her hooked.

"Will you wait for me?"

"Sure. Not much is happening here tonight, anyway. We can go to your place so you can change. Then we'll go to one of my favorite spots. But I won't tell you where until I know that you're serious about this."

I nursed my drink until she came back to the bar about a half an hour later wearing a plain, blue shirt and black pants. She appeared to be very tense, so I bought her a large cognac and watched her gulp it down nervously. That loosened her up quite a bit. During the entire taxi ride to her building in nearby Alexandria, Virginia, we joked and laughed and touched like old friends.

She was completely relaxed and more than a little giddy when we reached her apartment. Slightly off balance, she managed to open the door, strolled in, and put her purse on a small table near the entryway. I stood in the hallway, waiting for her to invite me into her home.

"What are you doing?" she asked. "Come in here and help me find something to wear!"

I entered, closed the door behind me, and followed her. As we walked through the dimly lit living room toward her bedroom, she kicked off her shoes and began unbuttoning her shirt. She dropped it on the floor just outside of the bedroom door. Inside the room, she flipped on the light and immediately stepped out of her pants and left them there. I stood in the doorway watching her.

Clothed only in a white, satin bra and panty set, she slid open the doors to her wall closet.

"Here," she said. "This is everything I've got. Tell me what you think."

As she walked the length of the closet, she swept her hand along the row of clothing and almost tripped over a shoe. I rushed over and grabbed her arm to steady her.

"All right," I said. "Show me your sexiest outfit."

She reached into the closet and pulled out a short, white, strapless dress in a clingy fabric. Holding it up against her body, she waited for my approval.

"Perfect. Put that on while I look for some jewelry to go with it."

I glanced around the room. There was a vanity with a small stool against one wall, the surface covered with cosmetics, perfumes, brushes, and jewelry. I immediately noticed the silver, decorative comb with uneven teeth. Picking it up, I looked over at Yvonne. She was twirling around in her little white dress, panties showing.

"So what do you think of it? When I bought it, the sales lady said, 'It has wonderful movement.'"

"It's very sexy, just like you." I walked toward her. "But you should wear your hair up so that everyone can see your bare neck and shoulders. We can use this beautiful comb. Where did you get it?"

I stood behind her, gathering her hair together and pulling it back. She became quiet and still as soon as I began touching her. I moved her hair to the left and exposed her smooth skin.

"Oh, I bought that a long time ago in New Orleans," she said in a soft, nervous voice. "I hardly ever use it."

Gently, I twisted her hair into a knot and slipped the comb in place. Then I put my hands on her shoulders and pulled her back against me.

Standing so close to her and feeling the energy that she was generating, my appetite took over. I almost expected to grow fangs, as I had seen so many times in the movies. I ran my tongue across the tips of my teeth, but they had not changed.

Still, I couldn't help but give in to my passion and put my mouth on her neck. I began gently kissing and sucking her warm skin, and she let me. But that wasn't enough. Without thinking, I found myself biting into her – hard – breaking the skin and releasing precious blood.

She cried out and tried to pull away from me, but I had a firm grip on her arms.

"Be quiet!" I said firmly and was surprised when she immediately grew silent. "Don't fight me."

She stopped struggling, and I dragged her over to the bed and pulled her into the middle of it. Blood had dripped down the front of her dress and was now trickling back off of her shoulder, blending in with the roses printed on her comforter.

As she lay there motionlessly with her eyes tightly shut, I squatted over her and tore at her throat with my teeth in utter abandon. As I lapped up her warm blood, I felt euphoric and completely alive. Every cell in my body was charged.

The pleasure of consuming necromantic energy for the first time was so overwhelming that I couldn't fully distinguish the many images and sensations that passed through my mind and body. All I can remember is feeling intense delight as I witnessed the misery of the animals that Yvonne had eaten. It was clear to me that the more they suffered, the more energy they created – and the more energy my prey had absorbed, the more gratification I experienced. In an instant, I realized that guilt, shame, and mercy were for fools. I was far above both humans and the animals they ate.

I ripped out Yvonne's throat and gulped down the blood. By the time that I was finished, she and I were both a bloody mess, but only one of us was still alive.

I removed my wet, sticky clothes and took a long shower in her bathroom. Yvonne and I were about the same size, so I was able to find a pair of leggings and a billowy shirt to wear home. I placed my own clothing in a plastic bag to dispose of later and left her body sprawled on the bed for someone else to clean up.

As I was about to leave, I turned back. I wanted to take her silver comb with me as a memento from my first meal.

During the taxi ride home, I thought through my hunting technique and decided that I would utilize the dating skills that I had honed in my former life to capture my prey. And I would use Yvonne's silver comb to make my meals more civilized.

In all of the years since that time, I rarely deviated from this formula. But with every meal, I grew increasingly disgusted with humans. I hated them all for their weakness and hypocrisy. Yet I had to eat, and necromantic energy was only found in the blood of humans. I surmised that it was probably a byproduct of the ability to make bad life-and-death decisions.

Anyway, it was Friday, about 8:45 pm, which was a good time to hunt. Resigned to do what I must, I put on a pair of black, wide-legged pants and a red, satin and lace camisole. As usual, I pulled my braided hair into a bun, held in place with my silver comb. Then I slipped into a pair of red, high-heeled sandals, grabbed my purse, and left my apartment to hunt.

I walked down the long, empty corridor and turned left into the lobby, where a slender man was entering the building carrying several plastic bags.

"Hey! How are you doing?" he asked, as if I were an old friend that he hadn't seen in months. His warm smile revealed perfect, bright white teeth.

I glared at him. "Do I know you?"

I was offended by his show of familiarity, but there was something about him that immediately caught my attention. It wasn't something that attracted me, just something that was out of place. I didn't know exactly what it was.

I took a good look at him. Probably in his late thirties or early forties, he had very dark skin and a very short hair cut. He was tall, and through his jeans and white tee shirt, I could tell that he was in excellent condition. Yet something was wrong that I couldn't quite pinpoint.

"Well, no, you don't know me, but I've seen you around the building a few times, always alone, for some inexplicable and inexcusable reason. Let me introduce myself: My name is Salaam."

He put his bags down and extended his right hand. In an unusual move for me, I shook his hand and introduced myself.

"You can call me 'Pearl,'" I said without thinking.

Why did I tell him my real name? I was slipping up because I was distracted. Well, it didn't really matter. He might be no more than my next meal.

"I don't know if you were about to leave or just came in the back door, but if you're not busy, why don't you come and have dinner with me? I just bought enough food to feed a family of twelve."

"I *was* going out, but I'm not in any rush."

"Excellent, Pearl. I'm in apartment 301," he said as we walked toward the elevators. "It's just an efficiency the size of a broom closet, but it works for me, and it's pretty cheap. Which apartment are you in?"

"I live on the first floor."

"Is it one of those split-level apartments?"

"Yes."

The elevator on the right arrived first. Once we got in, he put down the bags and pressed the button for the third floor. The spicy aroma of Salaam's carryout food quickly filled the small space.

"I'd love to see it sometime. I've been in a couple of other apartments like that in this building, and they're great – like mini townhomes. But the rent! I'm trying to live on as little money as possible, since I'm also trying to be as free as possible."

We walked down the hallway toward his place, and I wondered if I were doing the right thing. Slaughtering a man who lived in my own building could bring police attention that I didn't need. I wasn't concerned that DC's police department could actually capture me, but I didn't need the hassle. On the other hand, I wanted to know what it was about this man, Salaam, that perplexed me. In any case, I didn't have to make an immediate decision about my dinner. I would see where events led me and decide later.

"Here we are," he said as he opened the door to his apartment. "Welcome to my humble abode!"

I stepped in and was greeted by a slender, tiger-back cat who sidled up to me and rubbed against my leg.

"I hope you like cats. Obviously, Twiggy likes you."

I brushed away the fur that the cat had left on my pants leg.

"I don't mind them if they leave me alone."

I descended the half flight of stairs that led to the main room, and I saw a dark cat dart under the futon. Salaam followed me and placed his bags down in the middle of the floor.

"That was Two-Face. She'll warm up to you."

I said nothing.

"I hope you wouldn't mind removing your shoes. It helps keep the rug clean and, I hope, also makes your feet more comfortable."

I slipped off my sandals and placed them near the foot of the stairs. Salaam kicked off his basketball shoes and left them where they fell.

"You have such beautiful little feet! Do you wear such high heels all the time? Feet like those deserve to be pampered. And you should have a toe ring."

I smiled, slightly, but said nothing. He was more down to earth than most men I had dined on.

"Let me give you the grand tour," he offered, and we walked around the place, with Twiggy following close behind.

Well, he hadn't been exaggerating when he said that the efficiency was tiny. Beside the L-shaped main room, the apartment had a galley kitchen, a bathroom with a shower (there wasn't room for a tub), and a small balcony. He mentioned that there were two closets: a small reach-in closet at the foot of the stairs and a walk-in closet in the bedroom area.

In the living room, a denim-covered futon and a Papasan chair formed the seating area. A black and silver trunk was used as a coffee table, and the furniture grouping was anchored by a large, worn rug with a Southwestern pattern. A card table and two old Windsor chairs by the window served as the dining area. Designed as a space for a bed, the alcove instead held a beat-up, roll-top desk on which Salaam had placed his laptop computer and printer. A few mismatched bookcases were stuffed with books, records, and an old, suitcase-style record player.

His extensive collection of artwork on the walls and shelves consisted of carvings, paintings, and crafts from Africa and South America. The walls and blinds were standard apartment-building white, but the other colors in the room were earth tones: brown woods, green plants, russets, and blues. Two green, sun-bleached plastic chairs were on the balcony, along with a small container garden of herbs, tomatoes, and a few vegetables. The apartment was fairly neat, except for the desk area.

Salaam had furnished his entire home with obvious hand-me-downs and thrift store finds. The only items he had in abundance were books, record albums, and art.

"Well, that's it," he said with a sigh that was supposed to indicate that he was a bit embarrassed by his home, but it was clear that he wasn't.

I tossed my purse on the trunk and picked up a framed photograph that caught my eye. Displayed prominently on one of the bookshelves, it was a very old, black and white portrait of a plump but dignified-looking woman. Her hair was pressed and set in large waves, a style popular in the 40s or 50s, I supposed.

"Is this your mother?"

"Yes," he said, taking the picture from me and looking at it with a sad half smile. "I'm not embarrassed to admit that she was the love of my life."

Salaam put the photo back on the shelf and invited me to sit at the table while he prepared to serve dinner. The other cat, Two-Face, came out from under the futon and sat across the room in a corner watching me.

What a strange looking cat! She was predominately black, with random tan and orange speckles. But her face was divided almost perfectly down the center, with one side black and the other side mostly tan and orange.

"Usually, I cook, but on Fridays, I treat myself to take-out. This stuff comes from that Thai restaurant near 14th and U Streets. I hope you're open to vegan food. I can't pronounce the names of these dishes, but this one is stir-fried watercress in a hot chili bean sauce; this one is fried tofu sauteed with mixed vegetables in garlic sauce; and this one is tofu with ginger, onions, carrots, and broccoli in a bean sauce.

We also have vegetable fried rice and spring rolls. Oh, and my favorite, sweet and sour tofu."

I was only half listening to his ramblings about the food. Why should I care about the ethnic background of the food he was going to eat? As long as it contained meat, it didn't matter. My stomach was rumbling, and I needed to decide whether he would make a good meal for me.

"I'm not really hungry," I lied. "But you should go ahead and eat."

"Well, can I offer you something to drink?" he asked as he brought the bags into the kitchen and put them on the counter. "I have a bunch of different juices – cranberry, mango, peach nectar, orange, or," he opened the refrigerator and looked in, "a bottle of white wine that I've been saving for a special occasion."

"A glass of wine," I said with no intention of actually drinking it.

Still in the kitchen area, Salaam opened the wine, filled two glasses, and brought them over to the table. Then he returned to the kitchenette to prepare a plate of food for himself. Once everything was ready, we both sat down at the table.

"The kitchen's about to close. Are you sure you don't want any food?"

"I'm sure."

I swished the wine around in my glass. He began to eat.

"Oh, man! This food is excellent! You really should try it."

"It smells pretty good. What are you eating, anyway?"

"This is the sweet and sour tofu. It has onions, scallions, tomatoes, green peppers, cucumbers, and pineapple, in sweet and sour sauce."

"What type of meat is in there?" I glanced at my watch.

"None. I'm vegan."

This caught my attention. "What do you mean, 'vegan'?"

"I'm a very strict vegetarian. I don't eat meat or any animal products, such as eggs, dairy products, gelatin, or honey." He ate another forkful of food. "I also don't wear or otherwise use animal products – leather, fur, wool, silk, lanolin, pearls, etc. The only thing that's not vegan in this place is the cat food. I haven't been able to find a vegan solution for that."

This was one of the most ridiculous things I had heard in a long time. "Why?"

"Why am I vegan? Well," he said while still eating, "the short answer is that I want to minimize my contribution to the suffering of animals. If you're really interested, I can give you the long answer."

The telephone rang and startled both of us.

"I'll let my machine pick up."

Given the size of his apartment, it was impossible not to listen to the message as it was being left.

"Hey, No-Meat," a man's voice said. *"Where are you on this Friday night? Have you fallen off the wagon and gone back to your bad-ass ways? Don't expect me to believe that you have a date. You must be in the water closet, as usual. I keep tellin' you that you eat way too much fiber! I had another interesting ride home on the Metro today. A White guy and an Asian woman sat down in the seat in front of me, and next thing you know, they're practically – how shall I say – knockin' boots right there. Usually, I'm all for a good live show, but I had my daughter with me, so I tapped the guy on the shoulder and said, 'Look man, I didn't sign up for a front row seat at some type of Eurasian peep show. You need to take her home or to a hotel, motel, Holiday Inn...' I don't think he got the reference, or appreciated my advice, for that matter. At any rate, they stopped. Gimme a call. Later."*

Salaam smirked and rolled his eyes. "That's my friend, Lynford. Always the comedian, sometimes actually funny. I'll get back to him."

"He sounds charming," I said sarcastically. "Now, let's get back to this vegan thing. How long have you been vegan?"

"About thirty years now. Have you ever considered vegetarianism?"

"Of course not. People need to eat meat."

Salaam continued eating for a few moments in silence before saying, "Well, not according to the American Dietetic Association. Its experts say that vegan diets can actually prevent or treat certain diseases. Maybe you would enjoy learning more about it. You might be surprised how delicious vegan food can be. And you might discover that you like the idea as well as the results for your health, the animals, and the environment."

I looked at him blankly.

"Well, I haven't eaten anything from an animal since I was 22 years old, and I'm still kickin'. If you pull out your calculator and do the very complicated math, that makes me 52."

That surprised me. He looked much younger.

"But enough about me. I'd like to know more about you. If you don't mind my asking, how old are you?"

"I don't make a habit of telling people my age."

"Fair enough. So here's a less personal question. Where are you from?"

"I grew up in Brooklyn, went to college in Boston, moved around a bit, and ended up here."

"Do you like DC? Plan to stay?"

"I do like it and will stay as long as it continues to be comfortable."

I stood up and walked over to the futon. I sat down on one side, leaving plenty of room for him next to me. I still wasn't sure what I wanted to do, but if I were going to eat him, I needed to get him away from the table and closer to me.

"What do you do for a living?" He picked up his empty plate and took it into the kitchen.

"I make money through investments. You'd be amazed at how much money you can accumulate without actually making a product or delivering a service to anyone."

"Do you find that satisfying?" He stood in the doorway, leaning against the frame.

"Satisfying? It pays for the things that I want. That's the only reason I do it."

"Oh. Fair enough. I work as a fundraising consultant, writing grant proposals for nonprofit organizations, mostly in the fields of drug abuse prevention and treatment. It doesn't pay for much, but I do find it satisfying, and my flexible schedule allows me to pursue my other interests."

He paused, but I didn't ask him to elaborate.

"I love to read, sketch, and I play the guitar a little."

"I enjoy music. Why don't you put on a record? You've got enough of them!"

He went over to the bookcase that held his collection. Slowly, he ran his index finger across the spines of the albums that filled the third shelf. He stopped midway across and said, "Oh, I love this one, but I haven't listened to it in ages. Do you like Earth, Wind, and Fire?"

"They're all right."

"Are you familiar with 'New World Symphony'?"

"No. Let's hear it."

He removed the album from the shelf and took the record out of its beat-up jacket. Then he lifted the top of the suitcase-style record player and turned it on. Carefully, he placed the record on the spindle and the needle in the groove. Finally, he sat down on the other end of the futon, resting his back against its arm, legs crossed. The music started off with slow, African-inspired rhythms and the sounds of percussion instruments that I couldn't identify, ending in a crescendo after about ten minutes.

As the music played, he began to ask me questions again. "So tell me about yourself. Are you always so quiet, or are you purposely trying to be mysterious?"

I was surprised that he was so inquisitive about me. Most of my prey were usually only interested in talking about themselves and finding out what I could do for them.

"There's not much to tell. Come closer," I said.

"Why?" He looked genuinely concerned.

"I just want to get a better look at you." I added, "You don't look like you're in your fifties."

As he moved closer to me, I kneeled on the seat of the futon, facing him. I examined his face carefully and was startled by the openness in his eyes. I pulled him toward me by the shoulders.

"What are you doing?"

"I want to smell you," I lied. I actually wanted to sense his energy, which I now realized was somehow imperceptible to me.

"Why? Am I funky?" He pulled back and sniffed his underarms. Apparently satisfied that he didn't smell sweaty, he cupped his hand over his mouth to smell his breath.

"I just want to smell you." I pulled him toward me again. Putting my face near his neck and inhaling deeply, I still couldn't detect the presence of necromantic energy. It was as though he had already been drained. Apparently surprised and confused, he did nothing.

Equally bewildered, I whispered, primarily to myself, "What the hell...?"

"What?" He pulled away.

I became a little flustered, and I never get flustered.

"I didn't mean that the way it sounded. You just seem so different from every other man that I've met."

"Of course I'm different," he laughed. "I'm *very* different. If you take the time to get to know me, you may be amazed!"

Salaam was intriguing – but I was not curious enough to pursue this mystery any further. I looked at my watch and saw that it was already almost ten o'clock.

"Well, I'm not going to get to know you tonight. I've got to go," I said, picking up my purse. I was hungry, and he could not satisfy me, so I stood up to leave.

As he walked me to the door, he said, "I hope we'll get to know each other better. Especially being neighbors and what have you. Not because I think you're beautiful or anything like that..."

"If you take the time to get to know me," I said as I put on my sandals, "we'll both be amazed."

"Good night," he said as I stepped into the hallway.

"Good night," I replied as he closed the door.

Chapter 3

I left Salaam's apartment and went out into the hot, humid night. There were no stars; it was unusually dark, and I thought it would probably storm. The wind was blowing the trees about ominously, and a large paper cup bounced down the empty sidewalk.

I walked the half block or so to the corner and immediately hailed a yellow cab.

"Take me to The Labyrinth, that night club at 21st and M Streets."

I had been to The Labyrinth several times before and knew it would be easy to find an appropriate source of nourishment there. Plus, the club was only about a ten-minute drive from home, so I would not have long to wait.

Located in a renovated four-story townhouse in the Dupont Circle area, The Labyrinth was literally a maze, with numerous rooms that were interconnected. It had only been open for about a year, so it was still at the height of its popularity. When I arrived, the place was already jumping. Lights and shadows could be seen moving in all of the windows.

There was a queue outside, with about forty well-dressed people on it. Instead of walking right in as I had in the past, I decided to wait on line to see who else was going in. A fairly diverse mix of people had flocked there: about an equal number of men and women, most Black, most under thirty, but quite a few who were older. I preferred older men but didn't immediately see anyone of interest.

When I finally reached the entrance, I noticed a poster in the lobby advertising male and female "exotic dancers" that evening. *Good, I thought, that will make the hunt even easier.* I handed a $10 bill to the man at the door, a small price to pay for dinner.

As I made my way through the noisy crowd in the lobby, people instinctively moved out of my path. I entered the main room on the first level. The ambient lights were low, so low that you couldn't tell what color the walls were painted. Three or four spotlights randomly darted across the room. Hip hop music blasted, and a mob of twenty-somethings danced suggestively to the beat – the women in skimpy outfits and the men in clothing so large that it was impossible to determine what condition they were in: obese or emaciated. Every once in a while, one of the spotlights would illuminate the face of a young man or woman dancing to the pulsating rhythm. His or her eyes were invariably vacant.

The only seats in the room were half a dozen stools at the bar. They were already taken by a few lucky women who had managed to find some respite for their feet, pained from dancing in four-inch heels.

Looking around, I was not impressed with any of the men that I saw. They seemed too young to have accumulated the quantity of necromantic energy that I craved. Slowly, I walked across the dance floor and made it to the dimly lit stairs leading to the second floor. The stairwell was crowded with men and women trying to sweet talk each other over the din of the music. They stepped aside as I ascended.

The atmosphere upstairs was completely different. The disc jockey was playing dance hall reggae loudly, but it was not so loud as to be deafening. Most of the people on this floor were women, some young and very attractive, but quite a few who were trying to forestall the aging process by dressing too youthfully, and many who were overweight. They stood in small clusters, sipping glasses of wine and mixed drinks, looking around in anticipation, and occasionally leaning over to comment on what they were seeing and what they expected to see.

A catwalk had been erected across one side of the room, and several tables and chairs were arranged along the length of it. There was standing room only, and the women sitting close to the catwalk were talking and laughing comfortably, as though they were old timers.

The music faded, and a tall, buxom woman came out onto the runway wearing a tight fitting black tuxedo and a top hat. Surprisingly, she actually looked good in it.

"Ladies," she said in a loud voice into a microphone, then paused dramatically and looked around the room. "Ladies, do you know what time it is...? I said, do you know what time it is?"

The crowd shouted in reply, but each woman seemed to be shouting something different. The result was just noise.

"We have for you tonight one of the hottest male strippers in the Mid-Atlantic, in the Northeast, probably in the entire country." She looked down at a heavyset woman sitting with three other women at one of the tables near the catwalk. She was wearing a very gaudy gold sequined hat and matching blouse and held an old-fashioned glass, empty except for slivers of ice. "You know who I'm talking about, don't you?"

The robust woman stood up, grabbed the microphone out of the mistress of ceremonies' hand, and spoke into it. "I sure do, honey! It's got to be The Long Ranger!"

Visibly annoyed at having her thunder stolen, the mistress of ceremonies glared at the exuberant fan for a few seconds before regaining her composure. "That's right," she said, taking control of the microphone. "The Labyrinth is proud to present – the amazing, the incredible, the extremely well hung, the one and only – Long Ranger!"

Suddenly, reggae music was blaring from the sound system again. From out of the shadows behind the catwalk, a man leaped onto the stage. He was wearing a white cowboy hat and a black domino mask. His otherwise nude chest was partially covered by a tan leather vest that contrasted his chocolate brown skin. His muscular legs were clad in tan leather chaps over denim blue briefs and brown cowboy boots.

The women went crazy. Everyone started screaming. Those at the tables in the front stood up. The ones toward the back of the room pushed forward.

The Long Ranger began his routine by strolling down the full length of the catwalk, flexing his biceps and pecs and showing off his massive quadriceps. When he reached the end of the catwalk, he slowly removed his vest and turned around to make another trip across the stage. He dropped his vest on the catwalk, strutted to the center of the stage, and began unbuckling his chaps. The women went wild, some screaming, some laughing, and some briefly covering their eyes. With one hand, The Long Ranger pulled off his chaps and threw them to the floor. He was now wearing the hat and mask, briefs and boots.

I watched for a while, amused by the way that the women shrieked and screamed every time the stripper removed an article of clothing or gyrated on the stage. It was typical, ignorant human lust, set free by alcohol and the anonymity of the crowd.

Clearly, The Long Ranger spent many hours in the gym. His muscles were large and very well defined, and his dark skin looked smooth and flawless.

He walked to the other end of the stage and dropped down to the floor. The audience surged closer to get a better view. He did a few one-armed push-ups, to everyone's delight, and then turned over, sat on the floor, and slowly and dramatically removed his boots.

He stood up and tipped his hat to the crowd. Then he inched his briefs downward. The women screamed. He teasingly pulled his briefs back on, and the crowd let out a collective, "Aw!" The Long Ranger turned his back to the crowd and again began slowly inching his briefs down. This time, he did not stop. He eased the elastic waistband over his very round and very firm butt and revealed a white thong made of a loosely woven mesh fabric. The crowd roared as he spun around to face them dressed only in the white hat, black domino mask, and tiny white thong, which was practically see-through.

At this point, The Long Ranger jumped off of the makeshift stage and started to work the room, beginning with those at the tables closest to the catwalk, going from woman to woman, stroking himself, flexing, and gyrating until she slipped a dollar bill into his sweaty thong. Some of the women were glad to join in the routine. Those who ran their hands over his body or inserted their cash into his thong with flair were rewarded with a kiss on the cheek. The less vivacious women sat back in their chairs, watched him intensely – some almost clinically – and then tipped him. A few of the shy ones were aghast, covering their eyes with their hands, and trying to become invisible as he attempted to collect his tips.

Before The Long Ranger could make it over to where I was standing, I left, not wanting any physical contact with him. As I walked toward yet another staircase, which led to the third floor, the throng of women parted to allow me through. From the stairway, I could hear house music playing.

The main room on this floor was crowded with men watching a young woman who was apparently midway through her striptease when I arrived. I watched her for just a few moments. She was executing an elaborate routine quite skillfully, but she didn't look like she was enjoying herself. I wondered what had possessed her to choose this for a career?

Uncomfortable because the room was warmer and even more tightly packed than the others, I decided to venture up to the fourth floor. However, before I could make it to the stairs, I felt a hand on my arm.

"Excuse me," a man's voice spoke into my ear.

I turned around to see a short man of about forty-five staring back at me. He was light skinned, balding, and a bit plump, but very well dressed in a gray linen jacket, navy pants, and a light blue polo shirt. Most important, he radiated strong necromantic energy.

"This place is a little bit too wild for me," he said loudly over the sounds of the music and the crowd. "I was wondering if you could recommend a quieter night spot."

This was too easy. Is it even a hunt if your prey walks up to you, lies down, and plays dead? But he promised to be delicious and filling, so who was I to complain about my good fortune?

"I'm here on business for a few days," he explained, "and I really don't want to go back to the hotel. But this place is freaky!"

"Let's check out the fourth floor," I suggested. "Maybe it's better up there."

"Sounds like a plan. And by the way, my name is Ben."

Although the effort was unnecessary, I looked into his mind to find a name that would appeal to him. "I'm Serena."

"That's a beautiful name. It's my pleasure to meet you."

He took me by the hand, a gesture that I didn't appreciate, and walked toward the staircase. With him in the lead, this was no easy task. He needed to say, "pardon me," "excuse me," and "coming through," numerous times to get the men who were engrossed in the action on the stage to let us pass.

When we finally made it upstairs, we saw that there were several smaller rooms with a few loveseats in each. As in the rest of the club, the lighting was low. However, soft R&B was playing at a reasonable volume such that people could hold conversations. In two of the rooms, couples were necking, or more, on the sofas, so we chose a room that only had one other couple in it, talking.

Ben told me that he was from Chicago. He had been in DC for three days already and became bored staying in his hotel room alone each night. One of the room service waiters had suggested that he check out The Labyrinth, so here he was.

He worked as the business manager for a famous actor who, Ben claimed, would remain unnamed. Ben was in town working on a restaurant deal. He pulled out his wallet and showed me a few pictures of himself with various celebrities from the sports and entertainment industries.

I feigned excitement and agreed to go back to his hotel room with him to talk further. By this point, it was past midnight, and I was famished.

He was staying at the Barrington Hotel on 16th and K Streets, which was very nearby. We quickly caught a cab and were there in a few minutes.

The Barrington was a beautiful hotel, with the plush carpeting, ornate fixtures, and lovely furnishings that you would expect. It had undoubtedly witnessed its share of liaisons, but probably none like the one that was about to occur.

We took the elevator up to the seventh floor and walked down the hallway to his room. All the while, he was talking about the unnamed actor for whom he worked and dropping the names of the famous people he had met. Finally, we reached his door, and he invited me in.

"So, this is my home away from home. Make yourself comfortable."

I took off my shoes and sat down in the middle of one of the two full-size beds in the room.

"I didn't get a chance to eat dinner," he said. "What would you like from room service, Serena? They have late-night breakfast here."

"I'm not hungry. But you go ahead, please. Maybe I'll just have something to drink, a cup of coffee."

Nodding his head, Ben retrieved the Directory of Services from the nightstand and studied it before calling room service. He placed an order for my coffee and for a ham and cheese omelet with a side order of bacon and orange juice for himself.

"They said it should take fifteen to twenty minutes," he reported. "What can we do until then?"

"Tell me more about yourself. It seems like you've led a fascinating life, meeting all kinds of interesting people."

I wanted to keep him happy, and prey always enjoy talking about themselves, bragging about their accomplishments, pounding on their chests like gorillas. It puts them in a good mood, which is the humane thing to do for them on their last night.

"Okay. That'll be my pleasure!"

He prattled on for a while. I pretended to be impressed.

Eventually, he said, "Excuse me for a minute while I go to the little boys' room."

Once Ben was gone, I stood up to stretch my legs. Just at that moment, there was a knock at the door.

"Room service."

Ben was still in the bathroom, so I opened the door. Standing before me was a handsome man of Asian descent in an unflattering burgundy uniform. He was carrying a large tray.

"I'm here with your breakfast. May I come in?"

"That's what they pay you for. Put the tray on the bed."

He walked into the room but continued to hold the tray.

"Are you sure you don't want it on the desk? Something might spill."

"Whatever."

He put the tray on the desk and began arranging the silverware. It occurred to me that he was stalling. Maybe he hoped that I was interested in more than just breakfast.

He removed the metal cover that was keeping the entrée warm. The smell of bacon filled the room. "Is this what you ordered?"

"Yes, it is. Charge this meal to the room, and add a tip for yourself. Whatever you want."

"Thank you. That's very generous. I need you to sign this," he said, handing me the check.

As I was signing the bill, he commented, "That's a very nice outfit you're wearing. It really hugs your curves. Are you staying here alone?" He looked around for signs of a male presence, but Ben had left no obvious clues.

Ignoring his questions, I handed him the check and said, "Good-night."

He made one last effort. "My name is Ruben. If you need anything, anything at all, call room service and ask for me by name, Ruben."

I said nothing as he left, pulling the door behind him.

Ben came out of the bathroom.

"Was that our food?" He looked over at the desk and saw the tray. "Excellent! I'm so hungry, I could eat a horse! I hope you don't mind if we get right to it."

"Of course not. Go ahead and get started. I like a man who likes to eat."

He sat down at the desk and began buttering his toast.

"You're my kind of woman," he mumbled as he took a bite of the toast and put a forkful of omelette in his mouth. I walked over to the tray, put sugar and cream in the coffee, and picked up the cup. Marking time, I began slowly pacing back and forth in front of the beds, cradling the cup in both hands to warm them.

"How can I amuse you while you're eating?"

"I know," he said excitedly, a bit of food falling out of his mouth. "Tell me about one of your fantasies, what brings you pleasure. Something unusual but not so wild that it couldn't be done. Something that maybe you and I could do sometime down the road, if everything works out, and you wanted to."

Pretending to be shy, I said, "You would really want to hear that? I don't know if I could tell you. It's a little embarrassing, and I might shock you."

Still eating, he said, "Oh, now I really must know. I've got to hear it."

"OK. I'll try to tell you."

I put the coffee cup, still full, back on the tray and walked around the desk to where he was sitting. Standing behind him, I put my hand on his shoulder and whispered in his ear, "My fantasy is to tie a man down to the bed and dominate him."

He paused, smiled, and said, "Tell me more, please!" Then he went right back to eating, stuffing a whole strip of bacon in his mouth, along with another large piece of the omelette.

As I resumed my slow pacing in front of the beds, I again reached into his mind to find out what phrases would arouse him.

"Well," I began to speak slowly and softly. "In my fantasy, first I would get a warm, wet washcloth from the bathroom and give you a long sponge bath. I would wash your strong, muscular arms. I would rub down your bulging chest. I would stroke your rugged thighs, calves, and feet. And I would kiss and lick your entire body, from head to toe."

I walked over to the desk to see how much of this meal was left. He was just about done. "I don't think you need any more details."

"I don't think I can *stand* any more details!"

Now that he was finished eating, I was beginning to feel my own hunger rising up in me even stronger. I walked over to the bed furthest from the door and stretched out on top of the covers.

"It's a little cold in here. Come and warm me up."

He put in the last bit of food – a piece of toast – into his mouth, and said, "Just one second."

After wiping the grease and crumbs from his mouth with the napkin from the room service tray, he took off his shoes and joined me on the bed.

"Was your meal good?"

"It was pure pleasure! What's for dessert?"

Lying next to me, he pulled me toward him.

When he made a move to kiss my mouth, I turned my head, and let him kiss my neck instead.

"Why don't you just lie back and let me do the work?" I asked.

Slowly, I removed his shirt and pants while he was lying on the bed. Running my fingers through the hair on his chest, I put my face close to his large abdomen and inhaled deeply.

"Take it slow, or I'm not going to last!" he cautioned.

I continued to run my face up and down his torso. His necromantic energy made my entire body tingle. He pulled me toward his face, presumably to try to kiss me again.

"Wait a minute," I said. "Would you like to try something different?"

"If it's gonna feel good, I'm all for it!"

"Do you trust me?"

"Yes. Yes!"

I stood up and stepped out of my pants to reveal red panties that matched my camisole. A huge grin spread across his face. "You have a spectacular body!"

Ignoring his comment, I retrieved my purse from the other bed and took four long, black ribbons from it. I placed them next to Ben, climbed onto the bed, and kneeled on it by his side.

"What are those for?"

"I thought you said that you trust me! I'm going to tie you to the bed and have my way with you."

"I prefer bondage as a fantasy, not a reality. Let's do something else."

"Your cooperation is not optional. Play along."

"No. I'm not comfortable with this." He was beginning to get annoyed.

"Don't make a fuss." I forced his right arm to the corner of the bed. He tried to free himself of my grip.

"You're strong," he said. "But I'm stronger."

"Be still," I commanded, and against his will, he obeyed.

I tied his wrist to the headboard. He was unable to struggle but continued to protest.

"Wait a minute! I don't understand what's going on! Stop! I can't move! How are you doing this?"

I said nothing as I tied his other wrist to the headboard and one of his ankles to the footboard.

"You must have drugged me!" His voice grew louder. "You put drugs in my food while I was in the bathroom, and now you're going to rob me! Is that what you're about? I can't believe that I fell for your come-on!"

While I was securing his other ankle to the bed, I heard a soft knock on the door.

"Room service. I've come to pick up your tray."

Damn it! It was Ruben.

"Help me! Help me! She's trying to rob me!"

Ruben tried the doorknob and found that the lock had not been completely latched. Perhaps he had left it that way on purpose. The door opened easily, and he peeked in tentatively.

When Ruben saw Ben tied to the bed, he said, "Excuse me. I thought someone was in trouble."

"I *am* in trouble," Ben exclaimed. "Help me! She's a conniving thief who's trying to rob me!"

Ruben rushed into the room and pulled me backwards by the shoulders. I lost my balance and fell off of the bed.

"You'll pay for that!"

Before Ruben could even think about untying Ben's arms, I grabbed him from behind and placed him in a choke hold. Gasping for breath, he clawed at my arms, but my grip was firm. After a few moments, he lost consciousness. I continued to hold him as Ben watched helplessly in shock. Ruben's body went limp. When he collapsed onto the floor, I stepped over his body and headed to the open door.

I would not be interrupted again. I hung the "Do Not Disturb" sign on the knob before closing the door securely and locking it.

"Is he dead?" Ben whispered.

"Probably, but if not, I'll take care of him later." My attitude was matter of fact. "He shouldn't have tried to be a hero."

"Are you going to kill me?"

I kneeled beside him on the bed again. "Maybe. Maybe not."

"Oh God, how could this be happening to me," he moaned.

He got no sympathy from me. This was not what I had planned for the night either. I had wanted Ben high on endorphin, not in a state of terror. But there was no way to make that happen now.

"Please don't kill me! Listen. I have at least $500 in my wallet and a couple of thousand dollars hidden in this room. I'll show you where. You can have it all, just untie me."

"I don't want your money."

"Then I can help you become a model or an actress. I have the connections. You have the looks and talent. What do you say? I bet you always wanted to be rich and famous. You may never have this opportunity again!"

"I'm not interested in that. Just try to relax. I'm not going to hurt you. I like you. I'll be gentle. Everything's going to be fine." I began stroking his chest again, but he winced at my touch. He began weeping, and I realized there was no way to calm him at all.

"Close your eyes, and it will all be over soon."

He did.

I removed the comb from my hair, untied one of his arms, and quickly pierced the artery in his wrist with the comb's long teeth. Ben was no longer crying or moving at all.

Covering the wounds with my mouth, I drank the slow, steady stream of blood as it was released. It was a long, wonderful feast for me, lasting almost a half hour!

The first experiences that washed over me were the most delicious. I savored the fresh necromantic energy from his omelette. I could almost see the pain of the layer hen as the tip of her beak was clipped off before she was imprisoned in a huge building – a concentration camp – with tens of thousands of others like her. I sensed her suffering as she spent her short existence crammed into a small battery cage with seven other hens, the wire floor constantly digging into the skin on her feet, ammonia fumes from the urine-soaked cages constantly burning her eyes as she laid egg after unfertilized egg into the filthy enclosure.

As always, I also absorbed the energy from all of the other animals that had been a part of Ben's last meal and the meals before that. I became so full that I was actually exhausted, like I used to be after Thanksgiving dinner. I untied one of Ben's ankles and pushed his leg aside, making more room for me to sit on the edge of the bed. After relaxing for a while, I opened the television armoire, retrieved the remote control from the nightstand, and found a horror movie that looked interesting.

I stretched out on the bed next to my leftovers and watched the film until it was over at three o'clock. Finished for the night, I collected my ribbons and comb, dressed, and left the hotel. Even at that late hour, it was easy to catch a cab in front of the Barrington Hotel, so I was happily at home in about twenty minutes.

Chapter 4

About ten days later, I ran into Salaam again at the tenant mailboxes near the lobby. His mailbox door was open, and he was flipping through a stack of envelopes. Even in a simple sage green tee shirt and dark gray sweat pants, he looked pulled together. His clothes fit him, and he had a well-formed physique.

I wasn't hungry, but I was a bit bored, so I decided to engage in conversation with him.

"Hello, Salaam."

He noticed me and smiled. "Hey there, Pearl. How have you been? I haven't seen you around in awhile. What have you been up to?"

"Well, the night that I met you, I went to The Labyrinth." Just to gauge his reaction, I told him about the strippers. "Did you know that they have male and female exotic dancers there some nights of the week? That happened to be one of those nights. I didn't watch the female stripper's show, but I checked out one of the male strippers, and he was pretty talented."

"Really..." He didn't appear to be shocked or offended or particularly interested. "Strippers are not my thing. I used to find that sort of entertainment titillating, but not anymore. The price of getting older, I suppose."

"You seem to be so tame! You don't eat meat; you don't like strippers. Do you have some kind of religious basis for your asceticism?"

"Now, you've discovered my secret vice. Big words turn me on!" He grinned broadly. "But seriously, your question requires a long answer. Would you like to continue this conversation in my apartment?"

"All right. Let's go."

When we arrived at his door, the phone was ringing.

"Excuse me. I'll make it quick."

Salaam rushed down the stairs and over to his desk, tossed his mail on it, and answered the telephone. I followed him as far as the Papasan chair and sat down. That was a mistake. Its round shape and soft cushion forced me to practically fall back into it. I didn't want to be *that* relaxed. Immediately, I got up and sat at the table in a chair that would allow me sit up straight.

"Hi, Udah.... I can't talk right now. I have company.... Oh, okay. See you soon."

Salaam turned to me. "A couple of my friends are on their way over. They'll probably be here in about half an hour. I hope you'll stay and meet them."

"Perhaps."

He stood there for a moment looking at me. I was wearing a backless silk knit dress with a subtle geometric print on a navy blue background and bronze stiletto pumps, which I thought went well with the dress.

"Do you always wear such high heels?"

"You asked me that last time."

"I guess I have a foot fetish, yet another vice. Don't those shoes make your feet hurt?" Salaam walked toward me.

"I can take a little pain."

He kneeled on the floor in front of me and gently removed my shoes. Because I was seeking amusement, I allowed him to massage my feet for a little while. I was surprised by how good his hands felt.

"You really do have beautiful feet."

"And you've forgotten what we came here for." I repositioned myself, tucking my feet under the chair. Rebuffed, Salaam sighed and went to sit on the futon.

One of his cats, the lighter one, immediately approached me. She stopped in front of the chair, looked into my eyes, and then stood up on her hind legs, resting one of her front paws on the edge of the chair. She used her other paw to grab at my knee several times. I didn't know what to think. Was she trying to scratch me? Did she want me to get out of the chair so that she could sit there?

Sensing my confusion, Salaam explained. "You have to pay the Twiggy tax. She doesn't allow anyone to stay in this apartment for very long without petting her. If you rub her head or scratch her under the chin a couple of times, she'll leave you alone."

Reluctantly, I patted her on the head. That small gesture seemed to satisfy her need for acknowledgment, affection, and tactile pleasure all at once. Purring, she curled up into a ball on the floor near me and closed her eyes. I supposed that she now considered me to be her friend. She was pretty easy to befriend, just like Salaam, but the other cat was nowhere to be seen.

"Your cats are certainly different from each other. I thought that cats were all pretty much the same."

"Not at all. Each animal is an individual, based on genetics and experience, just like people. I found Twiggy in the alley behind the building when she was a kitten. She's only known kindness from humans, so she's always expecting the same. Two-Face, on the other hand, came to me by way of a friend who rescued her from an abusive woman. That's why it takes her so long to trust new people."

"Interesting..."

"Anyway, to answer your earlier question, I don't consider being vegan or other aspects of my life to be a form of self-denial. I don't want to eat meat, wear animal skins, etc. It's not a sacrifice to do what you want to do and what you feel is right. And I don't adhere to any particular religion. In fact, I'm agnostic. I do believe in most of the basic tenets shared by most religions: Ten Commandments, do-unto-others type of stuff."

"Is that the motivation for your veganism?"

"Yes, in part. All the religions that I know about frown upon violence. I'm most impressed with the Jain religion. One of its five basic principles is Ahimsa, or nonviolence. The point is to cause no harm to others, and 'others' includes all life forms – human, animal, and plant. While that may be impossible to achieve while you're alive – just walking down the street, you're gonna step on some insects –

serious followers of the religion do their best to minimize violence in action as well as in thought. In addition to not eating meat, they only eat plant foods that don't require killing the plant, such as fruit."

"Is that some Indian religion?"

Salaam nodded.

"You're not Indian, and you probably were raised Christian. The Bible is full of violence, and according to the Bible, Jesus ate fish. God gave humans permission to eat certain animals. Why have you turned your back on Christianity?"

Salaam stood up and walked over to one of his bookcases. He scanned the crowded shelves for a moment and then removed a book. It was a tattered copy of the Bible.

"For a long time, I did turn my back on Christianity, beginning when I was about 12 years old. There were just too many things that people had told me about it that just seemed wrong. The inferior position of women. Spare the rod, spoil the child. God's abuse of Job."

He returned to the futon.

"I tried to read the Bible myself a few times, but never got past Genesis. After I became vegetarian, I was at a conference, and one of the speakers from PETA pointed out that according to the Bible, God never intended for people to kill, abuse, and eat animals as they do. As a matter of fact, the second thing that God commands Adam and Eve to do after he created them – after he said, 'be fruitful and multiply' – is to be fruitarians. Listen to this passage from Genesis."

Salaam opened the Bible and quickly found what he was looking for.

"'And God said, Behold, I have given you every herb bearing seed, which is upon the face of all the earth, and every tree, in the which is the fruit of a tree yielding seed; to you it shall be for meat.'"

Though clearly no Bible scholar myself, I found it hard to believe what Salaam was saying. I went to sit beside him on the futon. I wanted to be able to read over his shoulder.

He continued, "God even commands animals to be herbivores. 'And to every beast of the earth, and to every fowl of the air, and to every thing that creepeth upon the earth, wherein there is life, I have given every green herb for meat...' So according to this, it clearly was not His will that we live by killing and eating our victims."

I was surprised by what he was saying to me. I wouldn't have believed that there was any support for veganism in the Bible, but there it was.

"Interesting," I said. "Since this is right at the very beginning of the Bible, I wonder why no one seems to have noticed it."

"Well, plenty of people have. But the Bible's a long book. People tend to pick and choose what suits them, including me! If I were Christian – and I don't claim to be – or a member of any other religion that accepts the Old Testament as holy scripture, I would tend to believe that what God originally said to humans was what he actually wanted them to do. A few paragraphs later, Adam and Eve are already sinning and getting kicked out of the Garden of Eden. So I think the later rules and regulations regarding eating animals with cloven hooves – or not eating animals with cloven hooves, I can never remember which – could be construed as God's compromise in dealing with the flawed beings that he had created."

Our discussion was abruptly interrupted by a long series of rhythmic knocks at the door.

"That must be Lynford and Udah. Excuse me for a second."

Salaam got up and went to open the door.

"Thelma or Willona?" Lynford asked Salaam as he strode through the doorway carrying a pizza box.

"Willona, of course," Salaam laughed.

They briefly embraced, and Lynford bounded down the stairs and kicked off his shoes.

Lynford was about six feet tall and probably about thirty pounds overweight. He wore a colorful, nylon tracksuit with too much embellishment – stripes down the sleeves and pant legs, company logos, mesh inserts, drawstrings, zippers, pockets, flaps, snaps – and a tee shirt beneath that was emblazoned with a huge Washington Redskins logo across the chest. His disheveled dreadlocks were just barely held back with a rubber band at the nape of his neck, and he smelled of cigarette smoke.

Until Lynford entered the small apartment, I hadn't noticed that the air was deadly calm. Now, it was charged and crackling. I could feel his necromantic energy from the other side of the room.

Making a much more dignified entrance, Udah followed close behind him, carrying a small, fabric purse and a shopping bag. She had a pretty face – large brown eyes and full, shapely lips. Her hair was styled in a free-form natural. She was wearing an embroidered peasant top with jeans and flip-flops. Lean, muscular, and tall, she looked as though she could have been Salaam's sister, but the obvious admiration in her eyes quickly removed any doubt about their relationship, or at least the relationship that she would have liked to have with him.

Udah and Salaam embraced.

"You look beautiful! I love this blouse. Yellow is definitely your color."

"Lookin' good yourself!" She stepped out of her shoes.

Lynford looked at me and asked, "J.J. or Buffalo Butt?"

Before I could respond, Udah shook her head in disgust. "Are they the only choices for women?"

"All right, all right! I'll throw in Ned the Wino," Lynford conceded as he tossed the pizza box onto the table.

"I'll take Keith, thank you very much," Udah replied.

"Who the hell is Keith?"

"Thelma's football player husband in the last season."

Salaam closed the door, and Udah sat down on the futon next to me, where Salaam had been a moment before. She placed her purse on the futon and the shopping bag on the floor. I didn't get a good sense of her necromantic energy, probably because Lynford's was so overwhelming.

"Pearl, these are my fellow Rhodes Scholars, Udah and Lynford."

Lynford stood before me and offered me his right hand. When I clasped his hand to shake it, he pulled me to my feet, stepped back, and briefly looked at me. Then he gave me a bear hug. I did not reciprocate. I was irritated.

Undeterred, he released me and said, "Salaam told me about you, but he didn't tell me that you were so fine. I guess he wanted to keep you for himself." In a stage whisper, he added, "You can do better."

"Lynford, shut up," Udah said. She turned to address me. "As you probably guessed by now, he's insane. I'm Udah. It's nice to meet you."

"Nice to meet you," I said to her as I returned to my original seat at the table.

Lynford and Udah sat on the futon.

"So what type of pizza did you bring?" Salaam asked as he peeked into the box.

"The works," Udah replied. "Onions, black olives, green peppers, sundried tomatoes, mushrooms, pineapple, and soy cheese."

"Excellent!"

"Disgusting," Lynford groused.

Salaam got plates and napkins from the kitchen and served everyone a slice, including me, despite my protestations. I put my plate on the table, refusing to taste the strange concoction.

Lynford picked everything off of his slice except for the onions and peppers. "I'm only eating this because I'm starving. Next time, we get real cheese, extra cheese, pepperoni, sausage, and ground beef."

"How do you know it's disgusting?" Salaam asked. "You've never even tasted it."

"It's fantastic," Udah said, "the way the juices of the sweet pineapple combine with the flavor of the olives when you bite into them together. And who doesn't like onions, green peppers, and tomatoes?"

"Me," Lynford replied. "And this soy cheese is slimy."

Salaam tried to compromise. "I'll admit that this particular brand of soy cheese doesn't melt very well. Maybe next time, we can get it without cheese."

"Okay," Udah said.

"Count me out," Lynford said. "Even without the soy cheese, it's still gonna be disgusting. Worse than disgusting! It's vulgar. They shouldn't even be allowed to call it pizza. It's an abomination. Pearl's with me on this, aren't you?"

I shrugged my shoulders, but the fact that I hadn't eaten any spoke volumes.

"Lynford," Salaam said, "your decades of eating meat and avoiding vegetables have gotten you what? Extra weight around the middle, high blood pressure, high cholesterol... You used to be a serious athlete!"

"The minor changes that you've noted are due to aging –"

"We're the same age, and I don't have those problems!" Salaam interjected.

"So blame it on the cigarettes, not meat. But I've still got plenty of performance in me where it counts! Right, Udah?"

"Ew!" Udah grimaced.

"You're hopeless." Salaam gave up and devoured his pizza where he was standing. When he was finished, he reclined in the Papasan chair.

"Anyway, back to the issue at hand," Lynford said. "I'll take Willona. Thelma's fine but too young for me. I always say, don't send a girl to do a woman's job."

"And that way, at least you'll have one adult in the room," Udah added.

Lynford rolled his eyes and continued. "You can tell a lot about people from the TV shows that they watch and the characters they like. That's my theory, and it's never been disproven."

"My mother likes to watch *Ellen*," Udah chimed in, "but my father complains through the entire show because Ellen's a lesbian. What does that tell you?"

"Given that tidbit and the other things that you've said about your father, it tells me that your mother probably wishes that she had been a lesbian, too," Lynford answered.

The three friends laughed. I simply observed.

"I've got a present for you," Udah said to Salaam, reaching into the shopping bag. "It's from Jamaica to add to your collection. I saw it in a little shop downtown and thought that it was something you would like."

She handed him a hideous wooden mask. It had exaggerated, flaring nostrils, a bulbous forehead, and large, wide teeth. Even though the eyes were merely cut-out spaces, they seemed to stare.

Salaam examined the artifact closely, but instead of saying, "Thanks, but no thanks," as I would have, he said, "This is really beautiful! Thank you. I love the detail. Look at the way that they even sculpted this guy's teeth!"

"Careful," Lynford said in a serious voice. "I bet it has some kind of evil Obeah powers."

"What's Obeah?" I asked.

"It's black magic of the Jamaican persuasion," Lynford explained. "Voodoo. Hoodoo. Juju. Witchcraft. The Black Arts. Sorcery. Necromancy. All that sort of thing."

"And, Salaam, you know what they say," Lynford turned to him and leaned forward, as though about to impart some great piece of wisdom. "'Never look a whore's gift in the mouth...' I mean, 'a gift horse in the mouth.'"

A huge grin spread across his face. It seemed that he had been waiting a long time for an opportunity to use that line.

Udah looked at him incredulously, her eyes opened wide. "I can't believe you said that!" She punched him in the arm.

"Ow!"

"Lynford, I think you've gone too far," Salaam defended Udah.

"I'm sorry. You know I'm just kidding. I can't help myself. Once a man and twice a child."

"Or in your case," Udah retorted, "once a child."

"Watch out, Salaam. Udah's gonna use that thing to watch your every move in this apartment. You had better blindfold it."

Ignoring Lynford, Salaam kissed Udah on the cheek and placed the mask on the card table.

"I'll find a good place to hang this later. Thank you!"

"Okay," Salaam returned to the Papasan chair and continued speaking. "Everyone seems to know that I enjoy collecting art. What about you, Pearl? What do you like to do when you're not working? Do you have any hobbies?"

For some strange reason, I felt the need to answer the question, but I wasn't going to answer it honestly. "I like to cook and sew. Nothing really exciting or esoteric."

"Let's get to the real deal." Lynford leaned forward, his elbows resting on his knees. "Are you in a relationship? Have you ever been married? Do you have any children?"

"No, no, and no."

"Do you want to be in a relationship? Are you taking applications?"

Quickly, Salaam jumped in. "Let's not put Pearl on the spot."

I could see that Udah was disappointed that I wasn't going to answer the question. Surely she was concerned that I would compete with her for Salaam's affections – and win.

She brought the focus back to Lynford. "And let's not forget who in this room is already married, Lynford."

"Hush, woman! Listen up," he said in a very serious tone. "I have something important to tell you. Something big. And very personal."

Even Udah gave him her full attention.

"You all see me as a happy-go-lucky type of guy, and I guess I am. But deep down inside, I'm very sensitive and in touch with my softer side. I haven't wanted to show it, but at the core, I have a very feminine sensibility."

He paused dramatically.

"In fact, I believe that I am a woman trapped in a man's body."

Salaam and Udah furrowed their eyebrows in bewilderment.

"You'll probably find it even more shocking when I tell you that the woman trapped inside of this very handsome man in front of you is actually a lesbian."

Salaam groaned. Udah shook her head. I sighed.

"So if either of you ladies is lesbian or bisexual or bi-curious or straight, for that matter, think about it. I can meet your needs like no other woman can."

Udah was the first to comment. "I should've known your 'true confession' would be nothing more than another scam to pick up women! What are you doing now, testing out your lines on us before launching them to the public?"

"Lynford," Salaam scolded, "you just say whatever comes to mind. It's all stream of consciousness with you. Your internal censor is asleep at the kill switch."

"That's not true. I don't have an internal censor. Fired him at least a couple of years ago. He was goldbricking, and I can live without that."

I didn't know what to make of these people or the nonsensical conversation, so I decided that it was time for me to leave. I had had enough live entertainment for the day.

"On that note, I think I'd better head home."

"Are you sure you don't want to stay and have some pizza? We haven't gotten to know much about you yet," Salaam said.

"Sorry, but I can't stay." In truth, I didn't want to stay. I hadn't engaged in this type of small-group, small talk in many, many years and had no desire to do it now. It was making me uncomfortable.

I put my shoes on and headed for the stairs.

"Good night," Udah said.

"I hope to see you again real soon," Lynford called after me.

"Good night," I replied.

Salaam walked me to the door. When we reached it, he whispered, "I hope Lynford didn't scare you off. That's just his way. He's actually a very nice guy once you get to know him."

"I'm sure your friends are wonderful, but I really do need to go."

"See you soon?"

"Perhaps."

I returned to my quiet, empty apartment and looked around as if seeing it for the first time. It was so similar yet so different from Salaam's.

Upon entering the apartment, instead of going down a half flight of stairs, you went up to the large, L-shaped living/dining room – the same size as Salaam's entire apartment. Passing through the dining area to the left, there was a spacious, eat-in kitchen that had been outfitted by the building's management with the latest appliances before I moved in – after a fire in that room had killed the previous tenant. Back through the living room, another short stairway led up to the full bathroom and two bedrooms. I slept in one bedroom and used the other as an office.

I had decorated the entire apartment with luxurious furnishings, including antiques, high-end electronic and computer equipment, and original artwork. Because I spent so much time here, I had spared no expense and had even convinced the management company to allow me to upgrade the light fixtures and add crown molding. My collections of books, music, and movies were extensive. I considered this to be the best living arrangement that I had ever created for myself.

But as elegant as my apartment was, as well furnished as it was, it lacked life. There were no plants, no cats, no friends dropping by, no admirer picking me up for a date, no lover arriving at midnight to while away the hours in bed. I never even received repairmen.

My experiences with Salaam had gotten me thinking. My home was a palace compared to his. The two apartments hardly belonged in the same neighborhood, let alone the same building. But he seemed to be completely satisfied with his place and with his life. He was happy every time that I saw him.

This piqued my curiosity. He was unlike the other men who served as my prey. They were always searching for pleasure, or consolation, usually through a sexual encounter with a woman who meant nothing to them, a woman who was a stranger. That was their downfall. But somehow, Salaam had achieved a level of contentment that others found elusive.

I began to feel very empty – and lonely.

For as long as I could remember, I had led a very solitary life, as a child, as an adult, and now. Humans hardly make good companion animals, and I never did like cats or dogs. Others like me are extremely rare, even though we can live for a hell of a long time, with a little care, but we make even worse companions than humans.

I decided a long time ago to amuse myself by creating an extravagant lifestyle. I set up my home as a testament to fine living, and I had not seen any reason to be dissatisfied until I met Salaam. My material wealth was starting to seem inadequate. I was actually beginning to desire personal interaction with another living being.

This was scary, and I don't scare easily.

Chapter 5

I had fallen into a lingering funk since my last encounter with Salaam. To overcome my melancholy mood, I had spent as much time as possible reading books about bloody wars, ruthless mobsters, and urban gang violence. These stories always lifted my mood, whetting my appetite for the kill.

Finally past my temporary misgivings about my lifestyle, it was time to hunt again. I wanted something different, so I sat down at my desk and opened my Internet browser. Immediately, I navigated to the site of *The Washington City Paper* and found their "What To Do" section. Tonight, I would focus on outdoor events; I wanted to dine *al fresco*. One announcement seemed perfect: an open-air concert at Fort Dupont Park in the Southeast quadrant of the city. Julio and Friends, a local Latin jazz/rhythm and blues band, was playing. The event description encouraged people to bring picnic dinners. I was certain that this meant plenty of fresh necromantic energy.

I printed out the directions to the park and went into my bedroom to change. My wardrobe was extensive, so it took me some time to decide. At last, I selected a red sundress with a tight bodice and a full, knee-length skirt. I matched it with a pair of low-heeled black sandals and slipped a trio of bracelets onto my arm. As always, I put my hair up in a knot, securing it with my silver comb. I was ready.

As I was descending the stairs, I heard a knock at my front door. I never received visitors, but occasionally, some imbecile would knock on my door when he was actually looking for another apartment. I usually didn't even bother to see who it was. However, I was about to leave, so I looked through the peephole. Salaam was standing there.

What the hell does he want? I thought. *And how did he discover which apartment I live in?*

I opened the door and saw that he was carrying a few large bags and had two boxes on the floor next to him. The boxes contained about six or seven small plants and a pair of large, decorative pots.

"Surprise!" he said, with a grin so wide that you would have thought he was offering me a rare treasure, rather than some dirt and weeds.

"What's all of this?"

"Last time I saw you, you mentioned that you like to cook. I brought you everything that you need to start an herb garden on your balcony. This way, you can have fresh basil, thyme, and rosemary for your creations. I also threw in a couple of flowering plants just to jazz things up."

"I'm not around much during the day to take care of something like this."

"It doesn't require much care, and you can water the plants at night. Are you going to invite me in?"

"I was getting ready to go out. I'll bring these things inside and put them together later."

His smile faded as he put the bags on the floor right next to where he stood.

"I thought we might be able to do this together, but I guess when you drop by unannounced, you get what you deserve."

"I guess so." After a moment, I felt the urge to add, "Well, thanks for the gift. It *was* a thoughtful idea."

"You're welcome. I hope you'll invite me over one day to visit the plants."

"Maybe, but I'm about to go out now."

"See you later," he said softly and walked toward the elevators.

Quickly, I made a few trips back and forth from the front door to the balcony to put the items outside. I was becoming irritated again. Salaam had a lot of nerve bringing me extra work to do and expecting me to be happy about it. My goal was to move the stuff from my doorway as fast as possible so that I could head out to the park. But for some reason, after I got everything onto the balcony, I decided to put the container garden together.

Not wanting to get my dress dirty, I went up to my bedroom closet to retrieve a bathrobe. I put it on over my clothes and thought about whether I had some gloves I could use to protect my hands. Unfortunately, I only had winter gloves. I decided to go ahead and use my bare hands to do the planting.

I emptied the boxes and bags and discovered that Salaam had thought of pretty much everything, including a small trowel, watering can, and yes, even a pair of women's gardening gloves.

Once I had arranged the two large, rectangular containers on either end of the balcony, I filled each one with potting soil. Carefully, I placed the plants into the containers, reading the instructions that came in the form of a tiny plastic marker in each pot. After filling the watering can in the kitchen, I drenched both pots and put a layer of mulch in each according to the directions, to prevent the water from evaporating too quickly.

When I stood back to look at what I had done, I actually felt proud. Although immature, the plants looked healthy, and the flowers had a pleasant scent. The greenery and the large pots spruced up the balcony which had previously been bare.

What am I doing? I thought. *I'm allowing Salaam to get me sidetracked again, just when I had finally gotten back into the mood to hunt.*

I took off the gardening gloves and tossed them on the pile of empty bags and boxes that I had created. It was time to find someone to eat. I went inside, removed my robe, and put it on one of the chairs in the dining room.

In the kitchen, I retrieved a picnic basket that I had purchased earlier that summer. The basket already contained a blanket, to which I added two crystal wine glasses, a few napkins, and a bottle of red wine. Basket in one hand, purse in the other, I left my apartment, got into my Lexus, and drove away.

Fort Dupont was a large park about thirty minutes from my home. Nestled within the well-tended landscape was a small amphitheater used for a free concert series that was held every summer. Tonight's band was already on stage, warming up on their instruments. The large lawn area in front of the stage was dotted with families and couples eager to enjoy a free performance. Fortunately, it was not overly crowded, and the night air was warm and still.

As I walked around looking for a man who could satisfy my needs, I spotted two men sitting on a blanket sharing a six pack of beer and a couple of large bags of fast food. The heavier and louder of the duo had curly black hair and a goatee. He was wearing one of those matching button-down, short-sleeve shirt and short sets that I hate so much – in a neon green pattern, no less. The other was tall and lean. He wore a blue muscle shirt and oversized denim shorts. He also had black hair, but it was straight and long, pulled back into a ponytail. From where I stood, I could see that they were looking around, shooting one liners at each other, and laughing. Clearly, they were checking out women and making lewd comments.

I walked over to an open area on the lawn between the two men and the bandstand. Not far from them, I put down my picnic basket and shook out my blanket. As they watched, I tossed my purse into the basket and took out the bottle of wine and one of the crystal wine glasses, clinking them against each other. Then I ran my other hand over the blanket, looking for a level area to set them down. Every movement that I made was deliberate and slightly exaggerated to attract the men's attention.

The curly-haired man asked, with a heavy Spanish accent, "Hey lady, are you gonna drink that whole bottle of wine by yourself?"

I sat down on the blanket facing him and gently smoothed out the skirt of my dress. Looking directly at him, I replied, "No. I don't intend to finish the whole bottle."

"Can we trade you some French fries for some wine?"

"No..." I said amiably.

"How about a hamburger?"

"No."

"Apple pie?"

I shook my head and smiled.

"Chicken nuggets?"

"Look, you can have a glass, no strings attached, if you just stop offering me food!" I laughed. "I'm not hungry."

He picked up one of the bags, brought it with him over to my blanket, and plopped down next to me. Once he was near me, I knew I had made an excellent choice. His necromantic energy made the hair on my arms stand up.

"I'm Arturo, and that's my cousin, Jesus."

"It's a pleasure to meet you." I nodded to his cousin, who was still sitting on their blanket, quietly observing us.

"And you are...?"

"...here to listen to the band."

He rolled his eyes. "I mean, what's your name?"

"Dolores." I smiled at my own joke – "Dolores" means "pains" in Spanish.

"Hey Dolores. It's no fun to watch the band all by yourself. I'll keep you company."

"That would be nice."

"Can Jesus come over here, too? He looks kinda lonely."

"The more the merrier."

"Jesus, *ven acá*," Arturo called to his cousin. "She says it's okay." Then he turned back to me, "He's kinda shy because he don't speak English too good."

Jesus came over to my blanket, carrying a beer and avoiding eye contact with me.

"This is Dolores."

"Hello," he said sheepishly and sat as far away from us as he could while still remaining on the blanket.

Taking a better look at them, I guessed that Arturo was in his late twenties, and Jesus was about ten years younger. Jesus was also radiating strong energy, but Arturo's was stronger, so I decided that he would be my next meal.

By now, the band had begun to play. We listened to the music in silence while Arturo ate his hamburger. Jesus sipped on his beer, and I toyed with my glass of wine. I would not make a move until they finished eating.

"So where's my wine?" Arturo finally broke the silence.

I took out the other crystal glass and poured some wine into it.

"Pretty fancy." He twirled the glass between his fingers, admiring the faceted surface before gulping down the wine. "You rich or something?"

"Something like that."

"So you like nice stuff? I just got me a new SUV with all the options. It's even got a Blu-ray/DVD player in the back. You ever seen anything like that?"

"No," I lied. "Never. Can I see it?"

"Come on. I'll show you. I'm parked real close."

He stood up abruptly, grabbed my hand, and pulled me to my feet, almost spilling my wine. He was tipsy from his beer combined with my wine. I hid my displeasure as he took the glass from me and gave it to Jesus.

"Hang on to this. We'll be right back."

I saw him wink at his cousin.

Still holding my hand, he led me to his vehicle, which was parked about a block away. It was one of the smaller models, metallic blue with silver pinstripes. We were approaching it from the back, so I could see that he had placed in the rear window a decal of a boy with a smirk on his face, urinating against a wall.

From clothing to car ornamentation, his taste was consistent, I thought.

He opened the rear door on the passenger side.

"Hop in."

I got into the SUV and slid across the seat to leave enough room for him to sit next to me. As soon as he was seated, he flipped a television screen down from the ceiling and said, "Look at this!"

I relaxed in the seat while he turned on a music video. I didn't recognize the group that was performing a lively song in Spanish. The lead singer was an athletically built man with undulating hips. Several skimpily dressed young ladies were backing him up.

"You see how clear the picture is? And check out the sound! *¿Chévere, verdad?*"

He turned the volume up, and we watched the video for a few minutes. I was surprised that for all of his previous forwardness, he now seemed afraid to do anything. Five minutes or so had elapsed, and

I was growing tired of playing his game, so I reached over and started unbuttoning his shirt, taking him by surprise.

"Hey, what're you doing?"

"That guy singing has such a hairy chest. It's very sexy. I want to see if your chest is hairy, too."

"Of course it is. Look." He undid the rest of the buttons.

I turned to face him and pulled his shirt back past his shoulders and off of his arms to reveal his naked torso. A mass of wiry black hair covered his chest and abdomen. He was not fit like the singer, but that was besides the point. I pulled my skirt up slightly and sat on his lap. His legs were between mine, and I was facing him. The aroma of beer and perspiration were strong on him.

"*¡Que rico!*" he murmured as I began peppering his neck and collar bone with light kisses. As I breathed in, my lungs tingled as though they were being filled with a thousand tiny charged particles.

He placed his hands on my hips, lifted me slightly, and slid his hips forward so that I was sitting on his groin. This movement caused my skirt to ride further up. His hands moved over my thighs to the hem of my dress and pushed it up to my waist. He began moving his hips in time to the music. Moving my pelvis in unison with his, I put both of my hands behind my head. I used the left one to hold my hair and the right one to remove the comb.

As I let my braids uncoil loosely around my neck, he said, "That's right. Let your hair down, *bebita*."

With the comb still in my right hand, I placed my hands on the seat back, at either side of his head, as though to steady myself. Distracted by the movement of my hips, he didn't notice when I pointed the long prongs of the comb directly at his jugular. I slowly but firmly pressed my weapon into his neck. Before he could react, I commanded him to be still. His body became motionless, but his eyes were staring at me.

Holding the comb into his neck and being careful to avoid getting blood on my clothing, I lowered him into a prone position across the seats. Finally, I pulled the comb out and placed it on the seat near his head. At the same time, I placed my lips on his throat and drank deeply of the rush of tainted blood that came forth. It was delicious.

I immediately began to take in the necromantic energy that it contained from the steer that had been ground into the hamburger that Arturo had just eaten.

Closing my eyes, I concentrated on images and sensations from the animal's two short years of life. After being castrated, having his horns violently removed, and being burned with a branding iron, he was allowed to graze in pastures with other cattle – for a while. After a time, he was prodded into a crowded metal truck. Confused and afraid, he watched in horror as some of the others were trampled or died from the heat during the long trip. When the truck stopped, he was forced into a building that reeked of death. Although hit with a stun gun, he was still conscious when the humans strung him up by his rear legs and cut off his head. The last thing he experienced was blinding pain that remained locked in his flesh as necromantic energy – until Arturo had absorbed it. Now, Arturo had surrendered it to me.

Humans called this "the circle of life," and what a circle it was!

When I was finished drinking, I wiped the blood off of my comb, using Arturo's shirt as a rag. I strolled back to the picnic area, comb still in hand. There, I found that Jesus had moved back to his own blanket but was finishing my bottle of wine. It looked like all of the food had also been consumed. I was no longer hungry, but I didn't like to let necromantic energy go to waste, so I decided to have Jesus for dessert.

"¿Dónde está Arturo?"

"He went to find a bathroom, baño, which might take him a while."

Jesus nodded. I sat on his blanket and put the comb down near me.

The band played a Gospel tune that I knew and liked – "I'm Going Up Yonder" – and I hummed along. Jesus listened quietly, his eyes darting about nervously. The band's next selection was a ballad that I didn't recognize or care to hear, so I made my next move.

I suggested that Jesus lie down to get more comfortable. At first, he didn't understand me, so I gently pushed him back by the shoulders until he lay stiffly on the blanket.

"Relax," I said softly and began rubbing his neck and shoulders. "You're so tense."

He remained silent, probably afraid that his cousin would return and be furious with him. Again, I would have to be the aggressor.

I bent over and kissed him lightly on his forehead. He looked shocked.

"*¡Arturo va a venir!*"

"No, he won't," I whispered in his ear. "It'll take him forever to find a bathroom. Anyway, I don't like Arturo. *No me gusta Arturo.* I like you. I told him that. *Él lo sabe.*"

It seemed that he understood me.

"*Ciérrese los ojos.*"

He closed his eyes.

"*No mueva.*"

He was paralyzed.

By this time, the band had been playing for at least an hour, so I figured that I had better move fast. I picked up the comb and quickly penetrated Jesus' carotid artery with it.

As I bent over him to consume his energy, a couple of preteen boys walked by. They pointed and snickered, believing that we were making love. The boys were no threat, so I turned my attention back to Jesus and the task at hand.

One of the last animals whose flesh he had eaten was a sow. What a bonus! Because pigs are such intelligent animals, the energy that they release is that much more delicious and robust. Unfortunately, I was already pretty full and only able to absorb a small portion of what Jesus had to offer: Flashes of the young pig's tail and teeth being cut off. Glimpses of her, years later, confined to a small pen, trying to nurse her offspring through the bars. Gut-wrenching despair as her babies were taken away after only a few weeks. I wanted more but just couldn't take it.

Fully sated, I arranged the bags from the fast food restaurant to cover the growing puddle of blood by Jesus' shoulder and arm. Then I folded my blanket and placed it, along with the two glasses and the empty wine bottle, back in my basket. I left the park and drove home before anyone realized that Jesus was neither drunk nor sleeping but dead.

Chapter 6

After devouring two men in one night, I should have been able to go for at least a full month without feeding again, but I was restless after only about two weeks. I guessed the cause wasn't really hunger. I didn't know what it was. My books didn't interest me. I'd seen everything in my extensive movie collection. I was tired of shopping online. That night, nothing seemed right.

As I walked aimlessly around my living room, a cricket began chirping loudly on my balcony. The damned insect had taken up residence in the plants that Salaam had given me. Every time I tried to kill it, it became quiet, and I couldn't find it. I went into the kitchen to search for a flashlight. I knew that there was one somewhere. After opening and closing a few drawers and cabinets, I found it. Tonight, I would kill that pest.

I slipped out onto the balcony. The air was particularly hot and humid outside, and I immediately wanted to go back into my air-conditioned apartment. But I was determined. I stood perfectly still, listening to the occasional car passing by and looking at the row of townhouses across the street. Then the cricket began to chirp again.

Moving as little as possible, I pointed the flashlight at the spot on the basil plant from which the noise was coming. The cricket kept on chirping. I moved closer, and it grew silent. Again, I waited, redirecting the light until I located the cricket sitting on the mulch at the base of the plant. After a few minutes, he began chirping again. I could see him rubbing his wings together to make the noise that he hoped would attract a female. I waved my hand at him, and he jumped or flew away, off of the balcony, hopefully to his death.

I returned to my living room, still restless. I paced the floors, tried rearranging the artwork in my living room, and then ascended the stairs to go to my bedroom. I looked around the room in frustration. The window treatments caught my attention. With the drapes open, the blinds seemed all wrong.

I hate these ugly mini blinds, I thought and jerked the cord.

Bad move. The blinds tumbled down in a mangled heap on the floor. The curtains were still intact, but I didn't want to risk any possibility of sunlight coming into the room in the morning. The blinds needed to go back up.

I could probably fix them myself, I thought, *but the night would be much more interesting if I asked Salaam to do it for me.*

A glance at the clock on the nightstand told me that it was about 1:00 am. Surely Salaam was in bed by now, but that didn't matter. I would wake him. Already wearing a black satin gown, I put on the matching lace robe and went up to his apartment, not caring that I was walking through the hallways in lingerie.

I knocked lightly on his door with my fist and waited, but he didn't answer. He must have been asleep. I rapped again using the metal door knocker and heard someone stumbling about inside. A few moments later, Salaam opened the door, bare-chested but wearing a pair of plaid pajama pants low on his hips.

Rubbing his eyes, he asked, "What's going on?"

"I need your help. The blinds in my bedroom have fallen down. Would you put them back up for me?"

"Your blinds...in the bedroom? Can't this wait until tomorrow?"

"No. I am obsessive about my privacy. I can't sleep like that. Anyone who happens to pass by could look into my room."

"I doubt that anyone is trying to peep into your bedroom at this hour... Not that you're not tempting, but I don't think your bedroom even faces the street. Does it?"

"No. It faces the alley, which is even worse. I need them back up tonight. Besides, you know that the blinds are required by building management, and I don't want them bothering me tomorrow. If you don't want to help me, just say so."

"I'll help you. Don't panic; I'll help you. Please wait here quietly. Udah is sleeping over." He went back inside.

While he rummaged around in the closet at the foot of the stairs, I stood at the open door wondering what I had interrupted. He came back carrying a toolbox and a stepladder.

"Okay, let's go," he said as he headed toward me. Then he paused. "Wait a minute. I need to put a shirt on."

He put his tools and the ladder down next to the front door and returned to the closet. He emerged wearing a cardigan.

We said nothing more on the way to my apartment. I believe that he was still annoyed that I was bothering him in the middle of the night with something that was not urgent, as far as he was concerned. But he was helping me anyway, so either he didn't mind very much, or he was more interested in spending time with me than with Udah, who was apparently already in his bed.

We took the elevator to the first floor and walked down the hall to my apartment. I unlocked the door and let him in. Now that he was here, I was actually feeling a bit nervous. He was the first visitor that I had ever had.

As he stepped inside, he suddenly became animated. "This is your place?! It's unbelievable!" He walked up the short staircase that led into the apartment.

It *was* impressive. The living area was furnished with an oversized sofa and matching loveseat upholstered in oxblood leather. Other furniture in the room included mahogany coffee and end tables, and a massive wall unit that housed a state-of-the-art home theater and audio system as well as leather-bound books and objects of art. The hardwood floors were exposed.

At the top of the stairs, Salaam exclaimed, "How'd you get management to agree to let you paint the walls this color? And look at all of this artwork!"

The walls were dark gold, and original artwork hung on almost every inch of space – mostly European-style landscapes, hunting scenes, and portraits of strangers' faces that I found interesting.

"Wow," he said, looking at my prized possession, a baby grand piano, which had been a major ordeal to get into the space. "You've got a piano! Do you play? This is too much!" He ran his hands over the dark wood and lifted the cover to look at the keys.

Salaam walked further into my home, into the dining area, and admired the antique furnishings – a heavy, ornate table and four matching chairs, also mahogany. The chair backs and seats were covered in a thick, ruby red brocade, and there was a matching runner on the table. In the center of the runner, I had placed a large, gold mesh bowl containing decorative glass spheres in various jewel tones. A dramatic crystal chandelier hung centered over the table.

"Does that mean you like my place?"

"It's fantastic, especially this piano! I always wanted to play but never learned how. Plus, pianos are so big and expensive, but this one fits in perfectly here. Can I go upstairs?"

"We'll have to. That's where the blinds are."

From the living room, another stairway led to a landing with three doors. On the left was my office. In the middle was the bathroom. On the right, my bedroom.

"Incredible," he said as we climbed the stairs. "This place is beautiful!"

We entered the bedroom, which was furnished as luxuriously as the rest of my home. The walls were chocolate brown, and gold drapes flanked the windows. The queen-size bed was covered by a red suede coverlet, and several pillows and neck rolls in various patterns that picked up the other colors in the room had been carefully arranged at the head of the bed. Beneath the bedspread were ivory silk sheets. The rectangular headboard was covered in black leather highlighted by a border of nailheads. A thick, Persian rug covered the floor on the side of the bed nearest the door. A set of matching antique lamps with strands of cultured pearls adorning the shades and bases had been positioned symmetrically on the nightstands. Across from the bed, there was another wall unit housing a second large-screen television, a home theater/audio system, my collection of movies, and more rare books.

"Did you decorate this whole apartment yourself? You must be doing really well trading stocks."

"You know, you ask a lot of questions but don't wait for answers."

"I'm sorry. I'm just surprised." He dropped his head, a little embarrassed. "Okay. Let's fix your blinds."

Salaam put his toolbox on the floor by the foot of the bed and set his ladder up by the window.

"I'll need you to serve as my lovely assistant," he said, climbing onto the ladder and examining the window frame for a moment.

"Fine."

"Well, to begin with, please pass me a small Phillips screwdriver..."

He worked on reinstalling the hardware that held up the blinds while I passed him tools, screws, and other bits that had come down.

Because Salaam was not tempting as a meal, I was able to focus on getting a really good look at him. Standing at the bottom of the ladder for that length of time, I noticed that he had a very small waist, flat midsection, and narrow hips. His waistband was slung so low that I could see some of his tightly wound hairs peeking out. I realized that he was not wearing anything under his pajama pants, and I was surprised to find that this aroused me. I was finding it difficult to stop staring, trying to see beyond the flannel fabric.

Salaam was completely unappetizing as prey – inert and bland – but I was beginning to find him appealing in ways that had not been important to me in a very long time. Strange.

Needing to distract myself, I finally said, "I can see why you're obsessed with feet. Yours are huge."

"You know what they say..."

"Don't say it."

"Big feet..."

"Watch it, now!"

"... big shoes."

I had to laugh, despite the fact that I had heard that joke before. It occurred to me that Salaam was pleasant to be around. Having him here had alleviated my boredom and put me in a better mood. It was a good thing that I hadn't killed him when we first met.

"So what's the story with Udah? Why's she at your place?"

"My, my! Aren't we curious tonight?"

"Yes," I said. "Afraid to answer the question?"

He smiled. "Of course not. Udah is feeling stressed because she's been put in charge of organizing her group's annual dinner. It's their biggest fundraiser of the year and an excellent opportunity for her, but it's also a huge responsibility. I promised to listen to her whenever she wanted to vent her frustrations or bounce ideas off of someone. I also told her that I would be her date for the event if she wanted me to go with her."

"Are you two a couple?"

"I've known her a long time, and we have a lot in common. You know, she's also vegan."

"Yeah, I thought so. But that can't be the entire attraction."

"No, but it *is* attractive."

"What else do you find attractive about her?"

"Isn't this getting a little personal?"

"I thought you were an open book."

"I never said anything like that! But all right. I'm going to tell you something that not too many people know about me and my relationship with Udah. Basically, she helped me turn my life around. I used to be much different than how I am now."

"How do you mean?"

"When I was in high school, I took a wrong turn, started selling drugs and much worse as the years went by."

"That's hard to believe."

"When I was at my lowest, my mother was murdered. It was – *is* – a tragedy, but her death saved my life, made me change. I quit what I was doing and left New York."

"What happened to her?"

"That's a story for another day." He took a deep breath. "Anyway, I moved to DC with practically no money and was living on the streets. One day, I saw a group of activists talking to people outside of a fast food restaurant. Curious and with nothing else to do, I went up to them to see what they were about. It turned out that they were members of an animal rights organization, and they were giving away free veggie burgers. I was starving, so of course I took several! That's how I met Udah. We ended up speaking to each other for at least an hour. The information that she shared with me about how animals are treated was compelling, but I was even more fascinated by her commitment to compassionate living as a vegan. Her lifestyle was the complete opposite of what I had been doing up to that point. It was kind of like

I found religion! So I guess she's been like a spiritual leader to me, in a strange way." He smiled.

A spiritual leader! I almost scoffed aloud at the idea but kept my skepticism to myself. I wanted to hear the rest of what Salaam had to say.

"She gave me some literature about her organization and wrote her phone number on it. I called her the next day, and over the next few weeks, she helped me get cleaned up and brought me to a community group that helps homeless people. They found me a place to live and a job, and I went back to school, eventually getting a bachelor's degree."

"Meanwhile, you and Udah built a relationship?"

"Udah and I have been friends ever since our first encounter, but we have never had a romance. When I met her, she was involved with some guy who never really appreciated her. Anyway, I wasn't ready for a relationship. I needed to work on my own issues without dragging Udah or any other woman into my life to make them miserable."

"That was then. What about now?"

"Does anyone ever finish working out their issues?"

"Are you trying to tell me that you haven't had a sexual relationship in all of these years?!"

"Only friendships."

"And you expect me to believe that? So why is Udah sleeping in your apartment tonight?"

He raised one eyebrow and looked at me as if to say, that's none of your business, but he took a deep breath and answered the question anyway. "We were up late talking, and it just didn't make sense for her to go home."

It was an interesting tale, but I wasn't convinced that it was the whole truth. I found it hard to believe that Udah was spending the night with him and there was no sex involved, especially because he was wearing almost nothing when he answered the door. He was probably just trying to keep his options open with me.

"Okay, I've got the hardware back in. Can you hold up the other end of the blinds while I put this end in?"

"Of course."

As he snapped the blinds back into place, he said, "Hey, wait a minute! I just realized that you have drapes. Why didn't you just close them? You don't need both the curtains *and* blinds for privacy."

"I told you. I'm obsessive. Curtains are not enough for me."

He just shook his head and rolled his eyes.

"Well, we're finished now. Since I'm already here, can I see the rest of your apartment?"

"Certainly."

He closed the ladder and picked up his tool box, taking one last, long look around the room. I had to wonder if he wanted to preserve the memory so that later, he could imagine himself here. We went into the hallway, and he placed his things at the top of the stairs.

"Here's the bathroom," I said, indicating the middle door.

"I'm expecting a glamour puss like you to have a fabulous one."

I opened the door, and he looked into the room, which was illuminated by the light in the hallway. The walls were painted black, in high contrast to the white tile. I had placed black votive candles in the four corners of the bathtub surround and on the large vanity counter. There was no shower curtain. A valance made of the same material as the runner on the dining room table completely hid the mirror on the medicine cabinet. That was the first thing Salaam noticed.

"Why's your mirror covered?"

"I don't need to see myself every time I walk into the bathroom. I already know what I look like."

"Wow. I've never heard anything like that before."

"Now, you have. You're not the only one allowed to have idiosyncrasies."

"You know, Jewish people cover their mirrors when someone in the family has died because during mourning, they're supposed to take a break from vanity."

"Well, I'm still as vain as ever. Do you want to see my office?"

"Sure."

We walked in, and I flipped on the light.

My office rivaled any office that might be found in a corporate environment. Yet despite the high-tech equipment, I achieved a classic feel through the placement of a traditional executive desk and wingback chair in the center of the room. In one corner, an armoire housed office supplies. In the other was a stand with a mid-sized television and audio system.

"Your office is better equipped than the place where I work, but aren't you concerned about being surrounded by so much electromagnetic energy?"

I turned my head sharply to look at him. For a second, I thought that he had said 'necromantic energy.'

"What are you talking about?"

"I'm sure you know that electrical equipment produces electromagnetic fields. Some people say they cause headaches, anxiety, depression, fatigue, nausea, loss of libido... Maybe it's the loss of libido that leads to all the other symptoms! Anyway, it's controversial."

"What proof is there?"

"The World Health Organization claims there's no scientific evidence that electromagnetic fields cause health problems. But the fact that scientists haven't found – or reported – any evidence doesn't prove that these fields are safe. By the way, I'm not trying to talk you out of your electronic equipment. I was just wondering if you're concerned about it. That's all."

Salaam had anticipated my irritation with his alarmist theories. He seemed to be intent on finding problems everywhere. I challenged him.

"As someone who seems to be pretty knowledgeable about health issues, aren't you concerned that you may be damaging your own health with your restrictive diet?"

"No, I'm not worried because I believe that I'm following the diet that's natural for humans. The human body isn't designed like that of a carnivore. We don't have fangs; our teeth are flat. We don't have claws; our nails are pretty much useless. Our saliva contains enzymes that help digest carbohydrates. A carnivore's doesn't."

"We've been using tools and weapons to get around the lack of fangs and claws for centuries."

"True, but there are also internal differences between humans and carnivores that make the digestion of meat problematic at best. A carnivore's stomach secretes bile that's ten times as acidic as a human's. Our small intestines are four times as long as a carnivore's, so meat has plenty of time to rot inside of our bodies. Not to mention that cholesterol – a major cause of death and disease in humans – is only found in meat and animal products. I could go on..."

"Look, even if your diet is 'natural,' it might not be nutritionally sound. What about protein, iron, calcium?"

"A reasonable vegan diet provides all of the nutrients that anybody would need. The only thing the vegans should to be especially vigilant about is vitamin B12. You only need a small amount, but it's essential for the nervous system to function properly. In a more natural world, we would get all we need from the germs and dirt in our food. But since we wash our hands and brush our teeth, or at least most of us do, vegans need to take supplements or eat enriched foods to make sure that we get enough."

"I think you're painting an overly rosy picture. If the vegan diet were so healthful, it would be popular among more than the fringes of society." At this point, I was just goading him on for the hell of it. Meat wasn't even a part of my diet!

"We may be the fringes, but we're the informed fringes. Potato chips and soda are incredibly popular, but that doesn't make them healthful." Salaam seemed to be getting a bit frustrated. "You know, there's a lot of nutritional propaganda put out there by people who want to sell you meat and cheese, even though they know they cause obesity, heart disease, high blood pressure, cancer, stroke, and diabetes. The meat and dairy industry puts billions of dollars into advertising. I wish the folks who sell healthy food had even a fraction of their marketing budget."

"You have an answer for everything, don't you?"

"Look, I really don't want to lecture you. I want to answer your questions and hopefully give you something to think about. I just get annoyed by the amount of suffering and damage being caused by misinformation floating around about what you need to eat. I hope I haven't overstepped. Anyway, it's late, and I'd better go."

We left my office in silence. He picked up his tools and ladder, and we walked downstairs toward the front door.

"Before I go, can I check out your kitchen?"

"Okay."

I guessed he was going to make one last effort to convert me by looking in my pantry. He was going to be surprised to find nothing there.

"I don't know if you'll ever invite me back."

"Neither do I."

I led him to the kitchen.

"It's so clean, but you didn't redo it like the rest of the apartment. And there's no food here," he said as he peeked into the refrigerator.

"I always eat out."

"I thought you said you like to cook!"

I shrugged my shoulders.

"You are truly a mystery," he said, shaking his head and smiling. "How's your herb garden doing?"

"See for yourself."

We went to the balcony. The sliding glass doors were along the long wall on the far side of the room, which consisted almost entirely of windows looking out onto Rhode Island Avenue. However, they were hidden by heavy sapphire blue drapes that I had hung over the management-mandated white blinds.

"These plants that you gave me have attracted an uninvited guest. A cricket has been living here, driving me crazy with its chirping every night. But earlier this evening, I chased it away."

"Whoops! Sorry about that. But everything looks great out here. I guess the cricket couldn't help but move in. Your balcony is very welcoming."

We stepped back into the apartment.

"And by the way, I forgot to mention how fetching you look in your nightie."

I had to smile. Who uses the word "fetching"?

"Are you trying to make up with me?"

"Yes. Is it working?"

"A little bit."

"Would I be pressing my luck if I asked you for your phone number?"

I hesitated but decided to give it to him. It would be better than having him come over unexpectedly again. I wrote my home number on a sheet of memo paper, neatly folded it in half, and handed it to him.

"I'm going to call you in a few days, once I know what my work schedule is going to be, to see if we can get together. I'd love to spend an afternoon with you."

"We'll see," I said as we walked back to the front door.

Buoyed by my softening attitude, he asked, "How about a thank-you hug?"

I embraced him briefly, resisting the temptation to press the full length of my body against him.

He smiled and said, "A friendly hug. That wasn't so bad, was it?"

"No, it wasn't," I answered truthfully.

Chapter 7

As promised, Salaam called me two days later, and I invited him to come back to my apartment the following week. He had made such a fuss over my piano that my own interest was reignited. The ability to create beautiful music was a talent that I had always admired. But without a naturally melodious singing voice, the only way for me to make music was to master an instrument. Piano was the obvious choice because I grew up with one in my home. I hadn't played in years, and my skills were pretty rusty. I found myself practicing for an hour or two every day, wanting to show off my musical talents for Salaam.

Playing the piano again took me back in time to when I was a child, studying piano with Mr. Martinez and preparing for a recital. The lessons were tedious, but now I was thankful that I could play. My favorite composition was *Rondo alla Turca* by Johann Friedrich Burgmuller. It was long, with a myriad of chords that were difficult for someone with hands as small as mine, but it was a lively piece that utilized the full keyboard. I wanted to play perfectly before my audience of one.

Shortly before Salaam was due to arrive, I went to my bedroom to get ready for our date. Expecting him to be dressed casually, I chose to wear my favorite jeans, which were comfortable yet hugged my curves. I paired them with a cream colored tank top, and I instinctively pulled my hair back and secured it with my comb.

Just as I finished dressing, I heard a knock at the front door. Salaam had shown up right on time, and I found myself to be as nervous as a little schoolgirl at her first recital. On my way downstairs to let him in, I realized that I wouldn't be needing my comb, so I pulled it out of my hair and placed it on one of the end tables in the living room.

When I opened the front door, Salaam was standing there, looking delicious in a blue, V-neck sweater and slim fitting jeans. He was holding a small bouquet of yellow roses and a box of chocolates. I couldn't believe it! No one had given me flowers and candy in an extremely long time, and it was endearing.

"Sweets for the sweet," he said, offering the gifts to me.

I took them from him. "What a nice surprise! Come in, and make yourself comfortable while I put the flowers in some water."

Before sitting down, he slowly walked around the living room, looking at the artwork hanging on my walls. I came back into the room from the kitchen carrying the box of chocolates and a vase with the flowers neatly arranged. I noticed that he was looking at the curtains, which were drawn, but he didn't make any comment about that. Instead, he paid me a compliment.

"You look really great. This is the first time that I've seen you dressed so casually. You're a natural beauty."

I smiled. "I didn't know that vegans eat chocolate."

"Dark chocolate is usually vegan, but I got these especially for you at a vegan store in Rockville. There are all kinds of fancy fillings in them – coconut, crunchy stuff, gooey stuff, whatever your pleasure. Let's try a few."

I put the vase of flowers and chocolates on the end table, and Salaam noticed the comb there.

"That's an interesting hair ornament. May I look at it?"

"Sure."

I handed it to him so that he could examine it more closely. Then I sat on the sofa next to him. Just to be polite, I opened the box of chocolates and took a small bite of one. "This is really good. I'm surprised." I ate the rest of it.

Salaam was still looking at my comb. "I like the simple, elegant design," he said as he sat down next to me. "Where did you get it?" He popped a chocolate into his mouth.

"It's an antique piece that I purchased in New Orleans a long time ago," I lied. "I was told that it belonged to an infamous madam who ran a brothel in the French Quarter at the turn of the century. I have no idea whether that's actually true. The shopkeeper probably just made up the story in order to sell the comb at a higher price. But anyway, I liked the comb and didn't really care what the history was."

"You know, it makes me think of the pick that I used to wear in my Afro back in the seventies. Of course, that was carved wood, not metal. I bought it in an African import shop in Harlem." He examined my comb's teeth. "My pick also had uneven teeth. I think they were broken, but I figured that just added to the character of the thing. The handle was in the shape of a lion's head with a wild looking mane."

"Yeah, I remember those days when everybody was running around sporting a big Afro with a pick sticking out of the back of it. People who wanted to stand out from the crowd and be individualistic positioned their pick in the side of their 'Fro. Funny how even nonconformists managed to find new standards to conform to."

Salaam chuckled at the memory. "Did you ever have a big Afro?"

"Of course! And cornrows. And marshmallow shoes. Do you remember those? They were simple shoes in all types of colors but with white soles and heels." Salaam nodded, and I added, "I also had a pair of Li'l Abners. Those were essentially construction boots, and mine were so comfortable that I wore them out, way down into the ground. The heels were almost nonexistent by the time that I finally threw them away!"

"Okay. I'm sorry, but as a man, I've got to ask. Did you wear hot pants? Tube tops? Hip huggers?"

"All of the above and halter tops, too. I've burned all the pictures from that decade. But it was fun teasing guys with those skimpy styles. Unfortunately, I eventually learned how easy it is to get guys going. It's not as much fun if it's no challenge."

Salaam laughed. "So I'm finally beginning to learn a little bit about you. You've been to New Orleans. You were old enough during the 70s to participate in those ridiculous fads. You used to be a tease. And you like flowers. What else do I need to know about you? Can you play the piano, or is it just for show?"

"It isn't just for show."

"Play something for me."

I went over to the piano, pulled out the bench, and uncovered the keys. I was happy to have a chance to show off but also afraid that I might not perform as well as I wanted to. After playing a few scales to warm up, I played *Rondo alla Turca* with no errors whatsoever.

"I'm impressed! You play like a professional, and that was no easy tune. You make me wish that I could play."

"Come over here, and I'll teach you an easy duet."

He came and sat beside me. On the small bench, we had no choice but to sit thigh to thigh. His leg, warm and firm against mine, demanded my attention. I wondered what his legs looked like unclothed.

Snap out of it, I said to myself, and then I played "Chopsticks" for him. I showed him a couple of chords to play with his left hand. His fingers were long and slender, so he had no trouble reaching the keys. Once he got the basics down, I suggested some ways that he could improvise. Finally, we put it all together.

As I played the melody, Salaam played the chords. He was a quick study. We played the tune several times, and each time, both he and I varied the way that we played our parts, but the music we created was harmonious. I was really enjoying myself.

"We're really jammin' now!" He laughed. "I can't believe that in only a few minutes you've got me playing the piano! You're really something else."

"When I was a kid, I used to play this same duet with my sister. It seemed like we could go on for hours."

Finally, we finished the song laughing, and he turned and put his arms around me. As we embraced, he nuzzled my neck and gently kissed my shoulder before releasing me. It felt good, and I wanted more, but this whole situation was so foreign to me that all I could do was pull away. He ignored my negative reaction.

"So Miss Pearl, you have a sister. Tell me about your family. Is it big? Small? Are you close?"

My mood became somber. I got up from the bench and sat on the couch. Salaam followed me.

"It was just me, my sister, and my mother. I don't know what the story was with my father. My mother never told us, and we never asked. I didn't have a close relationship with her. She worked two jobs, and when she was home, she was either sleeping or sitting in front of the television."

The long-suppressed memories were now vivid, and I felt a need to voice my frustration and disappointment with my childhood.

"My sister was much older than I, so most of the time, she acted more like a boss than a sister. We had some good times, especially at the piano, but I think she resented having to take care of me. We really didn't get along very well, especially the older and more independent I grew. We lost touch when she went away to college and never came back. Growing up, I felt like I didn't really have a family."

"That sounds kind of lonely. I wish things had been better for you. If your mother and sister are still living, maybe it's not too late for you to create new relationships with them. You're all older now and will probably understand each other's perspective better."

"I don't know where they are, and I don't want to find out. What about your family?"

"In my case, my brother, sister, and father all had serious run-ins with the law and were out of the house much of the time. But my mother was wonderful. She always tried to do the right thing, encouraged us to believe in ourselves and rise above the negative influences in our environment. And she was very affectionate and nonjudgmental. I always had to present a hard, unfeeling persona to everyone else just to make it through the day, but with my mother, I could be myself. When my father got locked up, I strutted around the neighborhood pretending that I was proud that he was a tough guy, but I would go home and cry in my mother's arms. I never had to worry that she would call me weak or childish."

"It must have been great to have someone like that to whom you could turn."

"Yeah, she really struggled to be a good mother and to give us a good home, but she just didn't have a way to do it. I thought that by selling drugs and making a lot of money, I could give her a better life. As it turned out, I only fattened my own wallet. She wouldn't accept what she called 'dirty money.' But she never gave up on me, no matter what I did, and what I did was get her killed." His eyes glistened with unshed tears.

"How?"

"I'm not ready to talk to you about that yet."

I had to accept that answer.

"It sounds like you still miss her."

"I think about her every day. Even if I live to be a hundred, I'll never stop missing her. I feel like I have a gaping wound that will never heal. The love of a parent can't be replaced. And when it's lost through violence, you never recover, no matter how old you are."

"Maybe it's a good thing that I never had that kind of love. I'll never know the pain that you're talking about."

My words belied my feelings. I actually was envious of the relationship that he described having with his mother, even if it ended tragically. As a small child, I hated not having a "real mom." My best friend Regina's mother was always hugging and kissing and doting on her when I visited their home. The only way that I could get my mother's arms around me was to pretend that I had fallen asleep on the couch so she would carry me to bed. And even though Regina's family was larger and had less money than mine, her mother always made sure that she had the latest toy or doll or, once she got a little older, the latest fashion craze that came along. I never got any of that, and I deserved it at least as much as she did. I did better in school; I stayed out of trouble; and I asked for less. I guess that's why I got less. I rarely even got any praise, which would have cost my family nothing. Anyway, I couldn't do anything about it, so that was that. Life isn't fair.

"Maybe you're right," he sighed. His words snapped me back to the present, and I realized that our conversation had taken a turn for the worse. I didn't want to rehash these painful memories.

"Well, speaking of love," he continued, "what's the story with your love life? Lynford asked you about it, but you didn't elaborate. Are you involved with someone?"

"Not exactly."

"What does that mean?"

"It's complicated, and I don't want to get into it."

I decided that I had had enough of this sentimentality that Salaam seemed to evoke in me practically every time that I saw him. I was ready to end our so-called date. I had been a fool to think that I could have any type of relationship with a human.

"Anyway," I looked at my watch, "I need to get ready to go to dinner."

A good hunt would set me straight.

"Do you want company? I don't have any plans."

"Sorry. I'm meeting someone."

"Wow." Salaam sat up straight. "Two dates in one day! That's pretty impressive."

"I like to keep myself occupied. So if you don't mind, I'll see you some other time."

"I'm going to take you up on that. I'm not easily discouraged, try as you may."

After escorting Salaam to the door and giving him a lukewarm goodbye, I went about the business of getting ready to dine out. I planned to put all thoughts of our time together out of my mind. Instead, I would focus on finding a good meal.

The incident with the blinds had given me the idea of stalking my prey at a home improvement center. I knew that there were always plenty of men there, drooling over the power tools and lumber.

I took off the light-colored top that I had chosen for my date with Salaam and put on a red midriff top. The Tool World near the Rhode Island Avenue Metrorail station wasn't far, so I drove there. I walked up and down the aisles, pretending to be searching for something. Finally, I zeroed in on my target in the gardening equipment aisle. He was about average height and weight, medium complexion, and bowlegged. He wore a drab polo shirt and faded khaki pants. Standing not far from the barbecue grills and accessories, he was looking at a lawnmower.

"Excuse me," I said as I approached him. "Do you know anything about barbecues?"

He looked up and then he looked me up and down. "Of course. I'm an expert. What would you like to know?"

"I like to cook a lot of different types of meat, pretty often – ribs, steak, chicken, burgers, you name it. Which is better, propane or charcoal?"

"Charcoal is much better for the barbecue flavor," he said with complete confidence.

"But what about the fat and blood dripping onto the briquettes? Can that start a fire?"

"No, no. It just adds to the aroma and the taste."

I moved closer to him and felt his energy flickering in the air around him.

"You know, I can't even think about this now, I'm so hungry. It's already so late, and I haven't had dinner yet. I wish I had a big, thick steak right now."

"No rabbit food? Good for you! You sound like my type of woman! I would join you, but unfortunately, I already ate."

"What did you have?"

"Veal parmigiana."

"That sounds delicious!" I was genuinely excited. He had just eaten part of a calf raised in the cruelest conditions: confined to a tiny crate to ensure soft, undeveloped muscles. The necromantic energy would be magnificent!

"Too bad," I continued. "I would have invited you to have a late dinner with me."

His face lit up. Glancing at his watch, he said, "Look, it's about 8:00 now. Call me at 10:00, and we can hook up." He pulled out his wallet and removed a business card. Handing it to me, he said, "That's my cell phone number."

I looked at the card and noticed that his name was Tom, and he was an accountant. The photograph on his card was pretty bad. It emphasized his receding hairline and overbite. He actually looked a lot better in person. Besides, his energy sparkled.

"I'm here with some people, so I've got to get moving. But promise that you'll call me at 10:00."

"I definitely will."

"I'll be waiting." He started to walk away, and then he turned back. "What's your name?"

"Judy."

I watched as he walked down to the far end of the aisle and disappeared into the corridor. I entered the parallel corridor at the other end of the aisle and followed him. He stopped in the lighting section and joined a woman who was already there shopping. She had with her a boy about three years old sitting in the child seat of the shopping cart. Both the woman and the child looked tired. She pointed out a couple of light fixtures, and together, Tom and the woman chose one and put it in the cart with their other selections.

"So he's a family man." I smiled to myself. "Not for long."

I walked around the store for another half hour or so, looking for other prospects. Not finding anyone better, I left Tool World and sat in my car for a while, watching customers going in and out of the store. I was amazed at how many people were shopping for home improvement supplies at this hour. It really didn't make any sense. Finally, at about 10:00 pm, I went to a nearby café and gave Tom a call.

He answered the phone on the second ring and said that he was going to be delayed. I was furious and let him know it.

"I've been wasting time waiting for you for two hours," I hissed at him. "You had better find a way to make it."

"I will, I promise." He paused for a moment to think. "Where are you now?"

"I'm still near Tool World."

"Meet me at my office building, in the lobby. The address is on my card. You know where it is?"

"Yes, I don't live far from there."

"Great. By the time you get to my building, I'll be there." He sounded nervous.

"Don't disappoint me."

"I won't."

I arrived at the Woodrow Building on 15th Street about fifteen minutes later. Through the glass doors, I could see that Tom was waiting for me in the lobby. He entered the vestibule and let me in.

"I'm really sorry about this," he said, looking down at his feet and avoiding eye contact with me. "I thought I could go through with this, but I can't. When you started talking to me in the store and seemed to be interested in me, it made me feel really good. To tell you the truth,

I saw you as a possible relief from some major problems that I'm going through. But I know this is not the answer."

"I don't know what you're talking about. Let's go to your office and you can explain. The vestibule is not an appropriate place for this conversation."

"You're right," he said and opened the inner door for me.

In silence, we took the elevator up to the fourth floor. The door to his office was directly in front of the elevators. He unlocked it and flipped the light switch on.

"Come on in."

I walked into his outer office. There was a waiting area with a large, traditional couch upholstered in brown leather, flanked by two matching armchairs. A coffee table covered with magazines was in front of the couch, and the receptionist's desk was on the opposite side of the room. I sat down on the couch.

He sat down next to me, cleared his throat, and began to speak. "I'm just having a really hard time. My wife and I bought a house that was a great deal because it needed a lot of work. We're renovating it now. But we've been unable to sell the house that we already owned, and now we're paying two mortgages."

I stared at him blankly, trying to figure out what all this had to do with me.

"On top of that, my son has sickle cell anemia and other health problems, and he had another crisis last week. The poor little guy was in such pain! The doctors don't think he will live much longer. My wife has had to take so much time off of work to care for him that she finally lost her job a couple of weeks ago."

I nodded my head, trying to look compassionate. He leaned forward, resting his elbows on his knees and hiding his face in his hands.

"I just couldn't take it any more and thought that spending some time with a beautiful, friendly woman like you would make me feel better. I'm sorry."

"It's okay," I said and put my arm around his shoulder. "We don't have to do anything you don't want to. I think you just need to relax for a while. Would you like a back rub? I think it will help to relieve some of your stress."

"Yeah, all right. Thank you for being so understanding."

I stood in front of him and pulled his polo shirt over his head. Then I pushed the coffee table back against the desk and knelt on the floor.

"Sit down in front of me. That's good. Bend your knees, and lean forward. There. You can lean your chest against your thighs."

He followed my instructions, and I began rubbing his back, making large circles over his shoulder blade area with the palms of my hands.

"That feels great."

I moved my hands lower and massaged the small of his back. He sighed as I swept my hands up his back to massage his neck and shoulders.

"Mmm," he murmured.

He began to speak more about his problems and depression. Strangely, I began to feel a bit sorry for him. This was spoiling the mood.

"Quiet now."

I placed my hands on the sides of his face and slowly moved his head in circles, clockwise then counterclockwise.

"This is wonderful. Do you do this for a living?"

"Something like that. Now close your eyes and keep very still and relaxed. I'm going to do something that you've never experienced before."

"Do whatever you want to do."

Still kneeling behind him, I removed the comb from my hair and gently pierced his neck. He let out a faint gasp, opened his eyes, and placed his hand on his neck.

"Hey!" he shouted as he looked at the blood on his hands.

"Be still," I commanded, and he obeyed.

Pressing my lips to his neck, I savored his blood. As the necromantic energy filled my being, I could sense the pain of the veal calf as he lay cramped in a wooden crate, trying to stretch his spindly legs and making small noises in an effort to call out to his mother – all to no avail.

Suddenly, I also had a vision of Tom's son suffering in a hospital bed and crying out for his father to come and comfort him. I straightened up and pulled away from Tom's body. He fell to the side, blood escaping from the wounds. I could see that it was draining onto the floor, being wasted, but I could not bring myself to eat. What was wrong with me?

As if in a daze, I got up from the floor, sat on the couch, and just stared at Tom for a long while, until the blood stopped flowing. Finally, I approached the body and pulled Tom's wallet out of his back pocket. It was bulging with pictures of his family; most were of his sickly son. I pulled out one of the pictures of the child and examined it closely before putting it in my pocket. I didn't know why, but I wanted to keep it. I threw the wallet on Tom's corpse and left the room quickly.

As I walked the six blocks home, I was completely unaware of what was going on around me. My senses didn't awaken until I entered my apartment and smelled the roses that Salaam had given me. And I could hear that the cricket was back again; it was chirping loudly.

I was now accustomed to the sound, and as silly as this may seem, I was glad to have the company. I just didn't want to be alone, haunted by images of Tom and his son and memories of my own lonely childhood. But I couldn't reach out to Salaam this time. It was too soon, and I was too shaken up.

Instead, I got on the Internet to read about crickets, what they eat, why they chirp, how long they live. I needed something to occupy my mind. I read page after page about crickets until I fell asleep at my desk, wondering why the cricket had chosen me. I knew it was probably just attracted to the plants, but there were plenty of other plants around. Why did it decide to make a home with someone like me?

Chapter 8

A few days had passed since my last meal, and I was still feeling uneasy about my prey and his son. Pacing back and forth in my bedroom, I thought that maybe it was because I had taken that damned photo from Tom's wallet. What a stupid thing to do! I walked over to the nightstand, opened the top drawer, and removed the picture. The little boy in green overalls stared at me with big, curious eyes. I crumpled him into a ball and threw him into the wastepaper basket. That didn't really help.

I went into the bathroom to wash my hands and face, and thought about what to do next. I wasn't hungry, but I was restless and, as difficult as it was to admit, still feeling lonely. Glancing at my watch, I saw that it was about seven o'clock. The sun had just about finished setting. I went downstairs and walked over to the sliding glass doors that led to the balcony. When I opened them, warm air rushed past my skin, and the previously muffled traffic noise became distinct. Immediately, I approached the basil plant and saw the cricket. It was just sitting there by itself, silent. Against my better judgment, I decided to go up to visit Salaam.

As I approached his apartment, I could hear the sounds of a conversation going on within. They weren't loud, but I could make out three voices. That wasn't good. I had expected to find Salaam alone and had wanted it that way. Using the door knocker, I tapped on the door anyway, and Salaam immediately opened it. As always, he was dressed comfortably in a T-shirt and sweat pants.

"Hi Pearl!" he said warmly. "Somehow, I knew it was you."

"I hope I'm not catching you at a bad time."

"Of course not. You're always welcome. Come on in."

Once again, Lynford's necromantic energy was a heavy presence that filled the room like steam in a sauna. He was sprawled out on the Papasan chair, his legs spread wide in a pair of distressed jeans. Udah was sitting in a more modest position on the futon, with the darker cat curled up on the lap of her pale blue shift dress. Her hair was braided in thick cornrows.

"Hey Pearl," Lynford said. "I was just asking No-Meat about you a little earlier."

"Hello," I said to both of them, taking a seat by the table while Salaam went to sit on the futon next to Udah.

A bowl of hummus and plate of pita bread triangles were on the trunk. Before sitting down, Salaam dipped a bit of pita bread into the hummus and invited me to have some. I declined the offer.

"Lynford, why do you call Salaam 'No-Meat'?" I asked.

"If I called him 'Salami,' I might offend his vegan sensibilities."

"What's wrong with calling him by his name?"

"Call him by his name...?" He thought for a moment. "Where's the sport in that? I need to be constantly challenged, on an intellectual tip. Anyway, Salaam is not his given name."

"No, it's my chosen name. As you know, it means 'peace,' a concept that you like to pretend you don't embrace."

"I'm not pretending. Just ask any of my ex-wives."

"Before you came in," Udah said, "we were talking about our past relationship disasters." She stroked the cat's head and back.

"Jackie, my second ex-wife, was the worst of the lot," Lynford said. "I have so many bad memories about *that* relationship – I can't even remember half of them!"

"She couldn't possibly have been worse than my ex-boyfriend," said Udah. "Bob. That's short for Beelzebub."

"What did he do that was so terrible?" Salaam asked.

"What didn't he do?!"

"If you had to narrow it down to one thing, what was the worst?"

"Well, it's humiliating. I don't know that I want to get into it."

"Come on now!" Lynford goaded her on. "I've shared all my dirt. It's time for you to return the favor. Spread the heartache around. Let me know that I'm not the only one with fatal distractions."

"I don't think so. It's too embarrassing."

Curious about Udah, I decided to join the conversation. I spent practically no time talking to women, and I wondered what Salaam saw in her. She seemed pretty dull to me.

I went over to the trunk and put some hummus on a piece of bread, just to make it seem like I was part of the group.

"I'd be interested in hearing your story," I said. "It might help me avoid the same mistake."

"Well, I don't know how instructive this will be, but I'll go ahead and tell the story that broke this camel's back. Everyone seems to want to know. But if any of you ever throws this back in my face – and by 'any of you,' I mean you, Lynford – I can't be held responsible for what I may do."

"I know how to counter your spells, Obeah woman," Lynford said. "Go on."

"Bob and I had been a couple for about three years. Our relationship was rocky, but for no good reason, we stayed together. He claimed that he loved me and wanted to be with me only. I was a sucker and did way too much to make him happy. For God's sake, I even cleaned his kitchen when it got to be too disgusting!"

"I need someone to clean out my car for me. Is Tuesday good for you?" Lynford quipped, but Udah ignored him.

"Toward the end of our relationship, my parents celebrated their 25th wedding anniversary. They have a really good marriage and decided to have a ceremony to renew their vows in front of their friends and family. They asked me to record the event because I have a camcorder."

"Uh-oh! I can see where this is going," Salaam said.

"Maybe you can. Maybe not." Udah took a deep breath. "Anyway, right after the ceremony, Bob asked me to marry him. It was all very romantic. Stupidly, I said yes. A few days later, I went over to his place with my camcorder because I wanted to talk to him about elements of my parents' ceremony that I wanted to include in our wedding. But we never got around to looking at the recording, so I left my camcorder there."

"So he recorded something over your tape?" Lynford asked. "That was his horrific crime?"

"No. He didn't record over the ceremony. It was a digital camcorder. But he did use it to record something. I found out from my mother. After a couple of weeks of waiting, she started nagging me about seeing the anniversary celebration. I took the camcorder back from Bob's apartment, and I guess he didn't realize that I took it, though I made no secret of it. Maybe he had already forgotten what he had done. Anyway, I gave the camcorder to my folks, and they gathered some of their friends together who had missed the big day. After they finished watching my parents' lovely, romantic ceremony, everyone got an eyeful of Bob having sex with some bimbo."

"Wow, that's deep," Lynford said. "How did you get your revenge on?"

"I don't do revenge, even if it's deserved. Like Gandhi said, 'An eye for an eye makes the whole world blind.'"

"And like I always say, 'If the whole world is blind, all those great handicapped parking spaces are up for grabs.'"

Salaam remained silent, a pensive expression on his face.

"What happened after that?" I asked.

"I ended it. Even if I had wanted to forgive him, there was no way that I could continue in a relationship with him. So it was over."

"Would you have wanted to forgive him?" I asked.

"I could forgive a man for having sex with someone else. When a man is unfaithful, it's normally to bring himself pleasure, not to hurt his wife or girlfriend. That's understandable and forgivable. What I can't forgive is a man sneaking around, lying, and generally making a fool of me. That's the ultimate display of disrespect and contempt."

Udah was on the verge of tears.

Salaam put his arm around her shoulders. "Let's change the subject."

"You all heard about those murders?" Lynford asked.

"You'll have to be a little more specific," I said. Salaam's other cat, Twiggy, came out of nowhere and rubbed against my leg before sitting on the floor at my feet.

"The ones where the men were being drained of blood, and it looked like they were killed while having sex – or at least trying to have sex." Lynford paused. "Come to think of it, it's probably hard to keep it up without any blood in your veins. Any who, I guess they were unfaithful, and someone gave them their comeuppance. Udah, that should give you some satisfaction."

"Don't be such an ass! How could I be happy that someone was murdered?" She glared at him.

Salaam tightened his grip on her shoulder, pulling her closer to him. Then he asked me,"Have you heard about those murders?"

I shook my head.

"I've heard about them," Udah said, "but not the details."

Salaam continued where Lynford had left off. "They found one guy lying on the floor in his apartment with two puncture wounds in his neck and most of the blood drained from his body. A few weeks later, they found a couple of guys in Fort Dupont Park – one in his SUV and his cousin on the lawn area in front of the amphitheater – both killed in the same way."

"You forgot about the guys that were found in the hotel room downtown before the two in the park," Lynford added.

"Oh, yeah. And most recently, there was that guy in the office building just a few blocks from here."

"I've seen some of the news coverage of these cases," Udah said. "What strikes me is that the police are so clueless."

"So Pearl, what's your theory? Salaam thinks it's got to be a female serial killer, but I'm not buying that," said Lynford. "There are practically no female serial killers in the history of this country. Women just don't have the killer instinct or testosterone or whatever it is that makes a person kill over and over again."

Before I could answer, Udah said, "What about the woman in Florida – I think it was Florida – who had a terrible childhood, ran away at fourteen, ended up becoming a prostitute, and started killing johns who tried to rob or rape her?"

"Well, prostitutes are a special breed unto themselves. The ones I've known were all a bit quirky."

"Lynford, you've actually paid women to have sex with you?" she asked.

"Of course not! After we had sex, I paid them to go away. But back to the point. That's only one female serial killer. There's always an exception that proves the rule. Can you think of any others?"

"No, but just because I don't know of them doesn't mean that they don't exist," Udah reasoned.

"Well, I think that you just don't want to acknowledge the obvious evidence that there is a vampire – probably female – out there preying on men," Lynford said.

"Oh, come on!" Udah rolled her eyes.

"You come on, Obeah woman! It should be obvious to a necromancing sorceress like you. There were clear signs that most, if not all, of the men were engaged in some type of sex play when they were killed, and they all had vampire bites on their necks – except the one guy in the hotel who was bitten on the wrist. It's a well-known fact that vampires seduce their victims before they –"

"'A well-known fact'! I don't know what world you're living in," Udah shook her head. "What do you think, Pearl?"

"To tell you the truth, I don't really see the difference between your two positions. Whether it's a female human killing the men or a female vampire killing the men, it would still be a female serial killer. What's the difference?"

"You're very diplomatic," Udah said with a hint of sarcasm in her voice.

"I think it makes a big difference," Lynford argued. "A human serial killer kills for various reasons: revenge, anger, jealousy, psychosis, etc. A vampire kills for food. It's an animal trying to survive. This makes the vampire morally superior."

"What are you talking about?" Salaam interjected. "If a person kills because of mental illness or extreme emotions, their diminished mental capacity makes them less responsible for their actions! That's how the law looks at it, and I think that makes the most sense. The person or vampire who kills for food has made a deliberate decision to kill in cold blood with no regard for the life or rights of the victim, just to satisfy her appetite. There's a higher level of culpability."

"Spoken like a true vegan," Lynford said. "I have to speak up on behalf of the carnivores."

"And I have to speak up on behalf of the ten *billion* animals killed in this country every year for food, and that number doesn't even include sea animals. *That* is truly mass murder."

"What if the vampire mesmerizes and seduces her prey in order to reduce its suffering?" I asked. "Isn't that humane? Is it a mitigating factor? I always thought that if men had their way, they would all want to die in bed."

"If I had to go, sex would be my method of choice," Lynford grinned.

"No matter what you do to sugar coat the facts or make the process of dying less painful, the victim still ends up losing his life. His family and friends end up losing him. I don't think anyone has the right to do that to another," Salaam said.

"Salaam tries to stretch this argument to cover animals as well," Lynford said to me, trying to pull me deeper into the argument. "I say human life is one thing; the life of an animal is something else."

"Who made you the judge of the relative importance of anyone else's life? A cow's life may not be important to you, but I'd bet it's as important to her as mine is to me and yours is to you," Salaam said.

"What about Lynford's argument about necessity?" I asked, actually beginning to enjoy this debate. "If the killer is a vampire and needs to eat men to survive, doesn't she have a right to self preservation?"

"Not by violating the rights of others," Salaam said. "And how do we even know that vampires actually need to eat people to survive? But instead of speculating about vampires, I'd rather stick to something we all know about: humans. Lynford would have you think that people eat animals due to necessity. But science has shown that eating meat and animal products is not only completely unnecessary, but leads to heart disease and other health problems. A vegan diet is much healthier."

"There's nothing you can say that will make me like vegetables," Lynford said. "And I can't live without meat."

"I guess you don't care that you're turning your body into a graveyard," Udah said.

"No, not really. It makes me more appealing to women who are into necrophilia."

"You can make these jokes because you're not a farmed animal," Salaam said. "You know, a philosopher argued that if you put ten people together and told them that they could end up being in any social position in society – a beggar, a ruler, a disabled person, a person of any race or gender – they would come up with fair and just laws, but you wouldn't necessarily get the same result if these people knew in advance what position they would be in. I think that's also true with regard to species."

"You know," Lynford said directly to me, clearly getting annoyed with Salaam and Udah. Slowly, he reached into his back pocket, pulled out a crumpled packet of cigarettes, and put one between his lips. "Salaam wasn't always such a goody two shoes," he mumbled, cigarette hanging from his lip. "This act impresses some of the ladies, but don't believe the hype. Udah has turned him into her clone."

"Come on, man," Salaam said. "It's all good."

"Yeah?" Suddenly, Lynford's demeanor changed drastically. He perked up and, out of the blue, began singing in an upbeat tempo. *"Yes, they're cousins. Identical cousins all the way. They laugh alike. They walk alike. At times they even talk alike. What a crazy pair."* He snapped his fingers, keeping time.

Udah asked, "What the hell are you singing?"

He took the unlit cigarette from his mouth. "The theme from *The Patty Duke Show*. You wouldn't know nothing 'bout that. Too young."

"A song about identical cousins?" she asked.

"A *show* about identical cousins. Salaam, you remember it. Patty Duke played Patty and Cathy. Patty grew up in Brooklyn, and Cathy grew up in England. Cathy came to live with Patty, and hijinks ensued."

"That's the most ridiculous premise I ever heard," Udah said. "How's it even possible to be identical cousins?"

"It's simple," I said. "A man has sex with his sister. She becomes pregnant with identical twin girls. The girls are not only twin sisters but also twin cousins."

"Deep," Salaam said. "I don't think the writers intended that interpretation."

Lynford continued the scenario that I suggested.

"Then, in complete shame and humiliation, the grandparents – there is only one set in this incestuous family – send the twins' mother and one of the girls to live in London. Sixteen years later, the girl returns, and the sister/cousins take out their revenge for all those years apart on the people around them, causing mayhem, destruction, grief, and despair."

Salaam laughed and said, "Hmm. I don't know about that last part. I seem to remember the show being a comedy."

"Use your imagination, man!" Lynford replied.

"This has got to be one of the most ridiculous conversations we've had yet," Udah said to him.

"If you can't stand the stink, get out of the bathroom!"

"It *is* time for me to head out," she said and turned her attention to the cat. "You'll have to get down now, Two-Face." Gently, she placed the cat on the futon. The cat immediately jumped to the floor and found a place to hide.

"Well, I'd love to chat with you all all night, but I gotta roll, too. The misses is waiting for me."

After Lynford and Udah left, I decided to probe further into Salaam's relationships. Having spent so much time alone for so many years, I found the nuances and inconsistencies to be fascinating. I sat on the futon and gestured for Salaam to sit beside me.

"You have an interesting friendship with Lynford. Obviously, you two are buddies, but there's also tension. He seems to harbor some hostility towards you."

"Lynford and I go way back. We grew up together, went to school together, and got into trouble together."

"You're glossing over all of the details. Something big must have happened between you two. What was it?"

Salaam leaned all the way into the futon, allowing his head to rest on its back. His eyes were closed and his body went limp, almost as though he were sleeping. Finally, he sighed, lifted his head, and began to speak softly and slowly.

"I told you before that I had a rough childhood. When I was growing up, my older brother and sister were in gangs, and my father was... Well, eventually, they all ended up incarcerated. My mother was dying of the myriad things that kill you when you're poor, while I stood by watching, unable to do anything about it. Lynford was there with me through it all. We were as tight as brothers, and if his younger sister, Karyn, had her way, we would have been brothers-in-law. She was always over at my mom's place. When I wasn't there, she would keep my mother company."

He shifted in his seat, turning to face me, with his arm resting on the futon.

"Even though I knew better, Lynford and I began selling drugs during our senior year of high school. My mother had always told me not to do it, but of course, I didn't listen. And I have to admit that I had a talent for it. Once I set my mind to doing something, I go for it full throttle, so I quickly became one of the most successful dealers in my territory. I had plenty of men under me, and that meant that I didn't have to get my hands dirty. And I never lived a flashy lifestyle, so I didn't attract too much police attention. Lynford ended up working for me, but I made sure he stayed away from anything too serious. He wasn't a very good dealer, but he was a friend, so I kept him around."

He took a deep breath and slowly released it.

"Are you sure you want to hear this?"

"Yes. Go on."

"Well, over the next few years, I changed dramatically, for the worse. I got greedy. Very greedy, and power-hungry. I was willing and able to crush anyone who got in my way. A few brave or foolhardy activists were always trying to fight drug trafficking in my neighborhood, and one woman, Joyce Johnson, was actually making headway. She almost single-handedly caused a dozen of my men to be locked up. The cops couldn't trace anything back to me, but I was furious. I ordered Jerry, one of my newest, youngest men, to kill her. I could tell by his body language that he didn't want to do it, but he was afraid to defy me. The next day, he returned and described to me in detail how he shot the woman and watched her suffer and die."

Salaam hung his head.

"Then he told me that she was his mother."

"Did this finally convince you to stop?"

"No. I acted like I didn't care. I told him that he was a grown man, and it was time for him to get off of the teat anyway. Then I pulled a wad of cash out of my pocket, peeled off three hundred-dollar bills, and stuffed them in his jacket pocket. A few hours later, one of my men burst into my apartment and told me that there had been trouble at my mother's house. Without waiting to hear more, I rushed over there. Mom lay dead on the kitchen floor. Blood was seeping out of gunshot wounds in her chest, and three hundred-dollar bills had been shoved into her mouth. Next to her on the floor lay the bodies of Lynford's sister and Jerry."

Salaam rubbed his temples as though he had a headache.

"To this day, Lynford can't decide whether he blames me or Jerry for Karyn's death. He can't decide if it's his own fault because he got into the business with me instead of trying to talk me out of it. He can't decide whether I've suffered enough already. He wants to hate me, but he can't. We're still like brothers. We share something that keeps us connected and pulls us apart at the same time."

The idea of trying to comfort him crossed my mind, but instead, I simply kept him talking. I wanted to learn more about his background.

"It's a little hard for me to understand how your life has gone from one extreme to the other."

"Well, there's more to the story. I promise to tell you one day but not now."

"I guess when you were younger, your biggest concern was creating an escape from poverty for yourself and your mother. What motivates you now?"

"I've adopted a 'do unto others' philosophy. I realize now that looking out for others rather than focusing on myself ultimately makes my life worth living regardless of my own circumstances. I think my mother understood that. It's also a way to try to make up for what I've done."

"What about God and the afterlife? Are you trying to go to heaven? Avoid hell?"

"I don't know whether God exists or if there is an afterlife, and I don't think it matters."

"Are you scared of dying?"

"No. If there is a God that metes out punishments and rewards... Well, I can't undo the wrong that I've done, I can only move forward in a better way. If that's not good enough, I'm just screwed. There's nothing that I can do about it. If there is no God that sits in judgement, it probably doesn't really matter what I've done, except to those who will reap the fruit of whatever good or bad I've brought into their lives. I can only control what I do now and in the future."

"Don't you want to enjoy what life has to offer?"

"Of course, and I do. I hang out with friends, read, watch television and movies, listen to music, and on and on. I've learned that I don't need a lot of money to enjoy life. More important than money is time, love, and companionship. Plus, I enjoy doing productive work that helps others. Even if I don't enjoy it in the moment, I feel satisfied and connected to other people when I'm finished."

"You seem to do a lot of thinking, and it's contagious. I'm going to go home now and think about what we talked about. You have an interesting way of looking at things."

I stood up to leave.

"You sure I can't convince you to stay?"

"No. I better go now."

When I returned to my apartment, there was no one there, as usual, but it smelled of the roses that Salaam had given me. As soon as I entered the living room, the cricket started chirping. It seemed as though it had been waiting to greet me, and I felt a little less alone.

Chapter 9

For the past few weeks, I had stayed away from Salaam. He called me several times and even knocked on my door once, but I didn't answer. Although I was strangely drawn to him, he had a disconcerting effect on me. He had made me think about childhood experiences that had been forgotten long ago and stirred up sentimental emotions that I didn't even realize I had within me.

I stepped out onto my balcony and watched the passersby. Rhode Island Avenue was a major street, so even at night, there were usually people there. Sometimes there were groups of four or five, going to or coming from an evening out. There were many tourists from the nearby hotels, often dragging their children around way past their bedtimes. I also saw couples out on dates. It was easy to differentiate the ones who were not yet well acquainted from the ones who were already in love or its aftermath, hate.

But I was most intrigued by the individuals who were walking alone. Why were they out at night by themselves? Were they on their way to a romantic tryst, or returning home from an encounter that had ended too soon? Maybe they had no one at home. I supposed they were walking about simply to be in the company of other humans, even if there were no interaction beyond asking someone for the time or how to get to a certain street. Perhaps their homes were dark and empty, so they preferred the busy and relatively well-lit streets.

My thoughts turned from the people outside to my encounter with Tom, and I blamed Salaam for my overreaction to the circumstances in which Tom's son found himself. All of Salaam's talk about compassion for food animals was causing my mind to play tricks on me. He was making me weak.

But now, I was beginning to feel hungry again, and I planned to enjoy the hunt and subsequent feast as much as ever. There would be no mercy. There would be no second thoughts. There would only be satisfaction of my desires.

I put on one of my sexiest hunting outfits. It was a short, red cocktail dress with spaghetti straps. The back was almost bare except for some very open latticework. The dress hugged my every curve. I donned a pair of four-inch, leopard print pumps and grabbed a matching clutch, just big enough to hold my keys and a couple of other essentials. Then I headed downstairs. It was Saturday night. I planned to go to a nightclub, find a man whose necromantic energy set him apart from the crowd, and consume him.

When I reached my living room, I was accosted by necromantic energy that was seeping into my apartment from the hallway like fumes. It was Lynford, and I opened the door before he knocked.

"Girl, look at you! You look so good, I could sop you up with a biscuit!"

"Hello, Lynford," I said in a friendly tone. Maybe it was time to taste him.

"I was concerned that nobody had heard from you in a while, but obviously, you are F-I-N-E – fine."

"You're looking good, yourself." For a change, he was actually dressed normally, in a gray, button-down shirt, black pinstriped trousers, and black dress shoes.

"I was going to surprise Salaam with an invitation to a house party, but I decided to stop by to see how you're doing first. It looks like you're going out."

"Yes, I am, but I'm not in a hurry. Why don't you come in for a minute?"

When he saw my apartment, his reaction was predictable – awe. I pretended to listen to his comments about my decor for a few minutes while I basked in his energy. It was appetizing. Then I steered the conversation in a different direction.

"Sit down on the sofa with me and tell me what's really on your mind. I know you didn't come here to talk about my decorating skills."

"Well, no. I came to throw my hat into the ring. You're a beautiful woman who says she doesn't have a man. For some reason, you seem to be interested in Salaam, so that says to me that you do want someone in your life. Well, forget about Salaam. I'm the man for you."

"Really?" I was amused by his forthrightness. I decided to play along. "But I find Salaam intriguing..." *Though not as appetizing as you,* I thought. *Would you like to be my next meal?*

"Yeah, he has that whole 'I'm a compassionate soul' thing going for him. But really, is that what you need? You can get that from one of your girlfriends. You strike me as a woman who needs a man who can get the job done. They say that a man is only as good as his tool. I've seen what's in Salaam's toolbox. It's half empty."

I forced a laugh and said, "I don't think you're being entirely truthful."

"Okay, okay. But you need a meat and potatoes type of guy. That's me. He's all wheat and tomatoes. Plus, I'm a slowpoke."

"You know, in my experience, men who brag about their sexual prowess tend to be the least capable."

"Not in this case. If you want, I can prove it to you right now." Using exaggerated movements, he began to unbuckle his belt.

"Just a minute! While that's a tempting offer, it's not what I had planned for the evening, and I'm just not that spontaneous."

"I already knew that 'spontaneity' is not your middle name. You and Salaam have been dancing around each other for, how many weeks now? And by the way, I'm not the only one who has noticed your slow and boring courtship. Udah isn't blind, you know, and she's been trying to get her hooks into Salaam for years."

"So what? If she can't hook him, that's her problem."

"Hold up now! Don't underestimate her. You've heard me call her an Obeah woman, haven't you? You think I'm just joking around? That woman knows some serious Voodoo. I'm certain of it."

"What makes you so sure?"

"Just look at what she's done to Salaam! Too bad you didn't know him before. He's a totally different person than what he was before he met her. I'm not talking about just slight changes. He's done a complete 360."

"You mean 180."

"Whatever. This isn't a geometry test. You get my point. For instance, he used to drool over sexy, stylish women like you. Women with skills. The more high maintenance, the better. And, like me, he had no problem getting them. Now, he pals around with this boring, granola chick who isn't even giving him any. Unless he's leading some secret life that I don't know about, he hasn't done the wild thing in years. Literally! I'm telling you, a person doesn't change that much, that quickly. It's unnatural. It's supernatural."

"Really..."

"Oh yeah! Udah's from Jamaica by way of Trinidad, and her ancestors were into some serious Obeah sorcery. They were famous for it, even beyond Trinidad and Jamaica's shores! My folks are from Barbados, and they've heard of her family, going back for generations. Her great granddaddy, Papa Niser, is even mentioned in an old Calypso song."

What a character! It seemed that Lynford would say anything to get into my bed. As tempting as his necromantic energy was, I wanted to find some other prey that could not be so easily traced back to me.

"I'll take what you've said under advisement, but don't get your hopes up."

"Just remember that I'm available to help you move past this doomed obsession with a eunuch. As Mae West said, 'The best way to get over a man is to get under a man.'"

"Okay," I said as I stood up. "It's time that we both leave."

We parted ways in the lobby. He stopped at the large mirror there to fiddle with his hair. He tied his dreadlocks back with a gaudy yellow ribbon, a throwback to his usual poor taste in clothing. I guessed that he would continue on to Salaam's apartment to try to convince Salaam to go with him to the house party.

I left the building and quickly caught a cab to Rendezvous, a nightclub in the Southwest quadrant of the city. When I arrived, I was disappointed to find that the place was not very crowded. I walked around for a bit, but I didn't sense any man who would fulfill me. I took a seat at the bar, waiting for someone interesting to enter.

While I was sitting there, a man came up beside me and asked the bartender for a Tom Collins.

"Hi there," he said to me. "Are you enjoying the music?"

"Not particularly."

"Yeah. This place is kind of dead tonight. It's usually jumping on a Saturday night. I don't know what happened. But you certainly brighten up the room."

"Not for long. I'm getting ready to move on."

"Me too. A friend of mine is having a party at his place tonight. I wasn't going to go, but that party has got to be better than what's happening here. Hey, I've got an idea. Why don't you come with me?"

I looked at him for a moment and inhaled deeply. He didn't have the energy that I craved. I wanted a meal, not a snack. But maybe I could find better prey at his friend's party.

"Why not? Let's go."

"Great," he said.

We exchanged introductions. He told me his name was Aubrey, and I introduced myself as Tonya. Being either frugal or a lush or both, he quickly downed his Tom Collins, and we rode in his car to the party, making inconsequential small talk along the way.

Our destination was a townhouse in a well-kept community just over the District line in Maryland. There were already many cars parked outside of the home, which I hoped was a sign that there would be someone inside to satisfy me.

We entered and found ourselves in the large living room area on the ground floor. The lights had been dimmed. Dance music was playing, and there were about ten people dancing in the middle of the room. A couple of sofas and several chairs had been arranged along two perpendicular walls, and most of the seats had been taken already. The third "wall" of the room was actually a breakfast bar that opened up into the kitchen. A wide variety of sodas and alcoholic beverages were on the bar, along with an ice bucket and glasses. Along the fourth wall was a stairway leading to the second floor.

"This is more like it," Aubrey said. "Let's get something to drink."

I walked with him over to the bar and poured myself a glass of red wine. He mixed himself a French Connection. I was surprised at how quickly he was able to drink such a strong cocktail, and he continued to drink heavily for the next half hour. We eventually found ourselves seated on the couch, where Aubrey proceeded to nod off. This gave me a good opportunity to look for someone else.

I was walking around the room to get a feel of each man's necromantic energy when I was approached by one of the partygoers. Dressed completely in black, he was of average height and probably around 35 years old. His skin and hair were ruddy; his cheeks were freckled; and his eyes were hazel. He was handsome in an unusual way, but I set my sights on him because he reeked of necromantic energy.

"Would you care to dance?"

I nodded and placed my glass of wine on the bar.

At this point, a ballad was playing, so he pulled me close to him.

"Are you here with someone?" I asked him.

"No. What about you?"

"Not with anyone who matters."

He pulled me even closer to him, his arms gently encircling my shoulders. As we rocked slowly from side to side in time with the music, he pressed himself against me, and I could feel that he was aroused. I deeply inhaled his scent, pressed the palms of my hands against his back, and slowly dragged them down to his waist. He placed his hands on my shoulders and, with his right hand, traced a line from my collarbone to the area between my breasts.

"You're really beautiful," he whispered in my ear. "And you've got a fantastic figure. I can't help but want to touch you."

"I want to touch you, too," I murmured, my lips gently brushing his cheek.

"Let's sneak upstairs to one of the bedrooms where we can have some privacy. You go first, and I'll join you in a couple of minutes. Go into the room right at the top of the stairs."

"Don't keep me waiting," I said as I slowly pulled away from his embrace.

No one seemed to notice me as I slipped upstairs, or maybe no one cared. I went into the room that my prey had mentioned and switched on the light. It was a small bedroom that was furnished adequately but without much style. I was more than a little disappointed at how messy it was. Nevertheless, it would do.

There were some clothes and women's magazines piled on the bed, which I quietly moved to the floor. Then I turned on a lamp at the far side of the room, switched off the overhead lights, and pulled the covers on the bed back. Just as I was finishing, my prey entered the room and locked the door.

"Good! You're here," he said. "I was afraid that I wouldn't find you, and we didn't get a chance to speak at all downstairs."

"Let's not waste any time on that," I said from my seat at the foot of the bed. "Someone could come at any minute. Take off your clothes and get into bed."

He raised his eyebrows and grinned, pulling his crew neck sweater over his head. Next, he removed his pants and shoes.

"Why aren't you getting undressed?" he asked me. "Aren't you going to join me?"

"I've already removed my thong," I lied. "That's all that's necessary."

He climbed into the middle of the bed, sitting with his legs stretched out in front of him. I kneeled on the bed beside him, facing him, and he smiled. I wanted to be especially ruthless, so I taunted him.

"You look absolutely delicious," I said.

"So do you, baby. Kiss me." He put his hand on my shoulder to pull me towards him, but I gently pushed it away.

"What did you have for dinner?"

"What?"

"I said, 'what did you have for dinner?'"

He looked at me with a puzzled expression on his face. "I don't know. I went to a restaurant. I guess I had salmon and some vegetables or something. Does it matter?"

"Are you in the habit of hopping in bed with women that you don't even know? What's my name?"

"Hey, you're the one who said, 'let's not waste any time.' I thought we might at least exchange our names and phone numbers."

He was getting angry and began to move as though he wanted to get up.

"Stay right where you are," I said, and he was unable to move. "You are nothing to me but a meal. I have no more feeling for you than you had for that fish on your plate earlier today. As far as I'm concerned, you have lived your life up until this point for only one purpose – to fuel me. I'm going to take from you what I need and leave the rest for your friends to clean up and dispose of however they see fit. I really don't care what they do with your corpse."

"What are you, some kind of psycho?" He tried to get up but could barely move. "What did you do to me?"

"It was nothing, really. Just a little food prep. Lie down."

He had no choice but to obey. I removed the comb from my hair and held it in front of his face so that he could get a good look at it.

"You know what this is? This is essentially my fork. Beautiful, isn't it? This is how I stay alive, and this is how you're going to die."

He was breathing heavily, and I could tell that his heart was racing. He was scared, panicked in fact, and I was determined to enjoy it. He was food, nothing more.

"If you're going to kill me," he whispered, "please let me pray before I die."

"What for? It's not going to help you any."

"Please!"

"Go ahead, but make it quick."

I was sure that he would beg God to have mercy on his soul or some such nonsense, but he surprised me.

"Dear Lord," he said, "please watch over Jean. She has always had my back, even though I never deserved it. If I had, I wouldn't be in this position now. So Lord, help her to find someone who will do right by her and who won't be as selfish as I know I've been. It's too late for me. Just please take care of her."

As he was speaking, I suddenly realized that if I were in his position, there would be no one in my life for whom I would pray. Even worse, there would be no one who would pray for me. Although I shouldn't have cared, I found this thought to be devastating, and I had to choke back tears. Still, I was determined to consume him. I couldn't be weak.

"All right. That's enough. It's over now."

He closed his eyes tightly, and I placed my comb at his neck. My hands were shaking as I thrust the teeth into him. In my haste, my aim was inaccurate, and I used too much force. His wind pipe was punctured, and he began making horrible gurgling noises as blood entered his lungs.

I looked at him, gasping and convulsing in his own blood like a fish suffocating on a ship's deck. I was unable to eat. I pulled the covers up over his body and watched the blood soak through the bedding.

Then I left the room quietly.

Tears were in my eyes as I descended the stairs. I didn't even know why I was crying, exactly. Maybe I was just too hungry to think straight. Maybe I was angry at myself for being weak. Maybe I was angry at my prey for revealing his best self, at the very end, when it was too late. Maybe he had revealed too much of me to me. I desperately needed to be in my own home.

When I reached the foot of the stairs, I was shocked to see that Lynford was at the party. His back was turned toward me, but I knew it was him. Even in the dim lights, I recognized that stupid yellow ribbon that held his dreadlocks. Even in the crowd, I could distinguish his necromantic energy. I could only hope that Salaam had not accompanied him.

I slipped out of the front door, unsure of whether Lynford had seen me. It had begun to drizzle, and the streets were dark and deserted. I realized that I didn't have a way to get home. How could I have planned this so poorly? I started walking in the rain, hoping that I would find a cab, a bus stop, or a train station. My feet began to ache, but I kept on walking. Finally, I found a major street, Landover Road, and was able to catch a bus to the Metrorail station. From there, I was lucky to get a cab home. The entire time, I tried to make my mind be still. I didn't want to think about anything. I didn't want to feel anything. But thoughts kept creeping into my consciousness anyway. I wanted someone to talk to, someone to comfort me, someone who would understand. But I had no one.

When I finally reached my apartment, I was drenched, hurting, and exhausted. I unlocked the door and went inside. It was silent. Too silent. I had become accustomed to the sound of the cricket chirping and immediately noticed its absence. Even though I was emotionally spent and my feet were on fire, I went out to the balcony with a flashlight to find the cricket. I saw him lying on his side under the basil plant.

He was dead, and I was completely alone.

Chapter 10

That night, I slept fitfully. I couldn't stop thinking about the man that I had just killed and hadn't even eaten. He was flawed, cheated on his girlfriend, and apparently was taking advantage of her generosity. But he also cared about her. I wondered what she was like. He had mentioned her name, Jean. Why did she put up with him? Was it because he was handsome, and she looked better with him on her arm? Did he make her friends envious? Maybe he was good in bed. They probably spent a lot of time together talking and sharing ordinary, everyday experiences. I'm sure he knew how she took her coffee. She knew where he kept his bills and how often he called his mother. Maybe they were making plans for the future, and he had promised himself to do better. Well, that wasn't going to happen. She no longer had him in her life. She was more like me now, alone.

I also thought about Tom and his family, especially his sickly son. The boy was now fatherless, adding to the burden of his illness. Did the family have health insurance? Was Tom's life insured? Maybe his wife would receive a large payment. Was it double indemnity for a case of homicide? No, that's for accidental death. What was his wife like? Did she have other children? Was she employed? Would she have to move in with her parents? What exactly had I done to her?

Too many questions and possibilities were running through my mind. I couldn't stop them, and I couldn't rest. I kept coming back to the idea that the men I had eaten, no matter how obnoxious, were each loved by someone and would be missed. I also kept thinking about the fact that if I disappeared tomorrow, no one would even notice.

I was miserable for the next several days, especially at night. It was too quiet without that damned cricket. It seemed to be the only creature who could stand me, and now it was dead. I was surrounded by death.

I was still incredibly hungry but didn't have the will to go out and hunt. I thought I was going to go crazy.

Finally, I decided to leave my apartment and visit the only person I knew who was almost a friend, Salaam. I held him responsible for planting the ideas in my mind that had turned my world upside down. He would help me deal with the consequences.

It was early evening. I forced myself to get out of bed and went into the bathroom to wash my face. As I stood in front of the sink, I paused to look at the valance that was covering the mirror. This was one time that I was really glad I didn't have to look at my reflection. I didn't want to see what I had become.

Once I started moving, I felt the need to hurry. I went into the bedroom and put on the first top and pair of pants that I came across. I didn't even bother to put on street shoes or fix my hair. I left my apartment in my slippers, smoothing my braids with my fingers as I was walking down the hallway.

By the time that I exited the elevator, I had convinced myself that Salaam would be happy to see me and that talking to him would make me feel better. Somehow, without even telling him what had happened, he would find the right words to help me make peace with myself and my situation.

But as I approached his apartment, I could sense that he was not alone. I stood a few paces from his door and listened. Udah was with him, and she was talking about me.

"I don't know why you're so concerned about her! That woman is cold, rude, and materialistic. She's nothing like you at all. She isn't vegan. She isn't spiritual. You didn't grow up with her, so there's no history or baggage to tie you two together. I don't understand your interest, unless..."

"Unless what? Unless I'm like every other man, drooling over a pretty woman in a sexy outfit regardless of her character? Is that what you want to say?"

"That's not what I was going to say, but maybe that's it."

"Udah, I don't like seeing you like this. Jealousy doesn't suit you. Pearl is no threat to our relationship. You and I have known each other for too many years, and I literally owe my life to you. You know that I love you."

I had heard enough. Obviously, turning to Salaam was no option. I walked slowly back to the elevator, not sure what I would do next. Almost in a daze, I went back to my apartment, undressed, and got back into bed. Thankfully, I finally fell into a deep sleep.

I was awakened by the unusual sound of my telephone ringing. I rarely received phone calls and wondered who it could be. As I picked up the receiver, I looked at the clock on the nightstand. It was about nine o'clock.

"Yes, who is it?"

"Hi, Pearl. It's Salaam. Will you come down to my apartment, please? I have something for you."

"I don't know. I'm not feeling too great."

"All the more reason for you to come over. I guarantee that I can make you feel better."

I thought about it for a moment and decided to go.

"I'll be there in a few minutes, but don't expect too much."

I hung up the phone and put my clothing back on, wondering what had happened between Salaam and Udah after I left his door only a couple of hours earlier. At that time, it sounded as though they were getting closer to each other and Salaam was distancing himself from me. By the time that I reached his apartment, I had decided that going there was a bad idea. There were too many unanswered questions, and things could get ugly. But just as I was turning to leave, he opened the door.

"Where are you going?" He grabbed my hand. "Come on inside. I have a present for you."

Reluctantly, I followed him into the apartment. The entire ambience had changed. Soft music was playing, and instead of the usual bright overhead light, the room was illuminated by four or five groups of candles throughout the room. Everything was neatly arranged. Salaam had hung the Jamaican mask that Udah had given him on the wall, its eyes dancing in the flickering light. His card table was covered with a blue tablecloth, and there was a small but beautiful bouquet of white flowers on it. The futon was made up as a bed and covered with a navy blue, faux fur bedspread. Both cats were curled up in the middle of it; as usual, Two-Face ran and hid when I came in.

"I like what you've done with your apartment. It's all very soothing – except for that eerie mask – but it makes me feel like I should have worn something more elegant."

"That can be easily remedied. Please make yourself comfortable, and I'll show you what I have for you."

I sat on the edge of the futon without saying a word. I was curious but still apprehensive. Maybe he was in the midst of implementing some type of seduction routine. I really wasn't in the mood to have another man lusting after my body, pawing at me, and trying to conquer me. Especially a man that I couldn't eat, for more reasons than one.

Salaam went to the closet at the foot of the stairs and removed a box that was beautifully gift wrapped.

"This is for you."

As he handed me the box, Twiggy came close to see what it was. Salaam stroked her back and gently placed her on the floor.

"What's the occasion?"

"I've just been thinking about you a lot lately. I was very disappointed that I've been unable to contact you for such a long time. Lynford mentioned that he saw you and that you were okay, but he's not the most perceptive guy in town. I suspected that you might be feeling down."

"I haven't been myself lately, but I'm okay."

"Well, let's see what's in the box. I think you'll like it."

I removed the ribbon and ripped off the red wrapping paper. Inside the box was an elegant robe in a green, blue, and gold paisley pattern. When I lifted the robe up to get a better look at it, I saw that there was also a small bottle of coconut scented massage oil in the box. I put the robe down on the futon and picked up the massage oil.

"What's this all about?"

"If you'll allow me, I would like to give you a hand and foot massage."

"Why?"

"Those are the areas where the energy enters and leaves your body. I promise that it will release the tension you're feeling, harmonize your energy flow, and lift your mood."

"I find it a little hard to believe that rubbing my hands and feet will do all that."

"It will only work if you're really able to relax. I'd like you to change into this robe and stretch out comfortably on the futon."

"Are you sure this isn't just some song and dance to get me into bed?"

"Trust me. I have no ulterior motives. I will only touch your hands and feet unless you ask me to do otherwise. And even if you ask me, I make no promises to go any further."

I decided to give him the benefit of the doubt and went to the bathroom to change into the robe that he had given me. The material was cool and smooth against my skin.

When I returned to the futon, Salaam was sitting on one side of it with the bottle of massage oil warming between his hands.

"You look beautiful in everything that you wear, but I think I told you that before. Let's begin."

I stretched out in the middle of the soft bedspread with my arms at my sides. Salaam kneeled next to me and picked up my left hand gently. Slowly, using both hands, he smoothed a small amount of the massage oil over the back of my hand, over my fingers, and into my palm. His hands were warm and soft, and the fragrance of the oil was delightful.

He continued the massage by gently applying pressure in a kneading motion to the fleshy areas on the heel of my hand, along the outer edge, and just below my fingers. Starting with my thumb, he softly rubbed, twisted, and pulled each of my fingers, ending by rubbing oil into my fingernails and cuticles. Gently, he laid my arm back on the futon, and repeated the massage on my left foot, right foot, and right hand. When he was finished, he lay down quietly next to me.

The massage was wonderful. I hadn't been touched that way by anyone, ever. Who would have guessed that it would have felt so good? I was completely relaxed and wanted to open up to him. I felt that I could talk to him about what was troubling me, and he would understand.

"I want to tell you about something, but you have to promise me that you won't laugh."

"Of course I won't laugh. What is it?"

"Part of the reason that I've been sad is because of the cricket that was living in the plants that you gave me. I think I told you about it. At first, its chirping was a terrible annoyance to me, but I eventually got used to it. Well, the cricket died, and now I miss it."

"What you're telling me isn't silly at all. It shows me that you have a soft, sensitive side. The cricket was a unique little life that chose to enter your world. He was attracted to your balcony because you took that little piece of bare concrete and put some lush, living plants there. That tiny cricket appreciated what you did and showed his appreciation by moving in and creating a comfortable home for himself."

"Well, now it's dead."

"I don't know how long crickets live, but I doubt that it's more than a month or so. It *is* sad that the cricket is dead, but he lived out his natural life span in a green oasis despite being on a busy city street. That's a beautiful thing. He was one lucky cricket."

"I guess you're right. But its death has got me thinking about the meaning of life, my life in particular. After all, the cricket served no purpose. It didn't seem to do anything besides eat, sleep, and chirp. To tell you the truth, my life isn't much different, aside from the chirping part. What's the point, really?"

"You're a beautiful, sexy woman. You have a fantastic apartment. You make plenty of money without even having to leave your home. I thought those were the things that were important to you."

"I guess our conversations over the past few months have had an impact on me. I've begun to feel that my life has been meaningless. I'm living the good life, but I don't believe this is a good life that I'm living. I don't know that my life is worth living. I don't know if it needs to be ended or just changed."

Salaam moved closer to me on the futon and put his hand on my shoulder.

"The thoughts that you're having now are upsetting, but I think that ultimately they will lead you to a better place. Your eyes are opening. You're beginning to take a critical look at values and habits that you've been taking for granted for a very long time. Self reflection is always a good thing."

"I don't know about that. I don't know if I can change what I am, and I don't know what I would become. I don't know what to believe in."

I began to weep silently, and Salaam pulled me close to him and held me.

"Pearl," he whispered. "I believe that you will be happy once you turn your focus away from self gratification and toward the universal life force that connects us all. We are all one, including you, me, and that cricket that you're mourning. It's the reason that you're mourning."

I turned away from him so that he wouldn't see me cry, but I pressed my back against the front of his body. I wanted to feel his warmth, and I wanted him to continue to hold me.

"I think that the two of us are a lot alike. I was unable to find happiness until I adopted an approach to life based on principles of compassion and being intentional, deliberate, and thoughtful about my actions and how they affect not only myself, but others, including people and creatures that I don't even know. I knew that if I were trying to be vegan just for selfish reasons – to avoid illnesses or to avoid the wrath of God – I would probably succumb to internal and external pressures."

"That sounds good, but I don't know if I can do it or even if I want to. You and I are not the same. Believe me, I have some concerns that you never even thought about."

"I'm not saying it would be easy, but if you internalize the importance of caring about the well-being of others and how your actions affect them, I am positive that you can do it. I would love to help you."

Listening to his words as I was lying there in his arms, I seriously considered changing. It would be wonderful to have this kind of connection with someone all of the time. It was beautiful the way that Salaam's cats showed their affection for him. I would love to have people and even animals treat me that way.

But I am what I am, I thought. *If I don't continue to consume necromantic energy, I will cease to be. Maybe that's the only answer. Death by veganism.*

Salaam and I lay there without speaking for a long time. Eventually, he fell asleep. I wanted desperately to be closer to him, but I didn't know what to do. He rolled over onto his back, and that gave me an opportunity to sit up and look at him sleeping by candlelight. He was a beautiful man, and I wanted to have him in my life. I made a vow to myself to accept his offer of help and strive to change. If we were successful, everything would be different and better. If we failed, I would be no worse off.

Without waking him, I got off of the futon and removed the robe he had given me. I folded it neatly and put it on the table next to the flowers. Then I went to the bathroom to retrieve my clothing and get dressed. When I went back into the living room, Salaam was still sleeping soundly with Two-Face resting near his head and Twiggy at his feet. I blew out all of the candles and left his apartment quietly.

What a difference a couple of hours had made! I was feeling cared for and optimistic. I had someone on my side who had helped me see everything in a different light. As I walked toward the elevator, I was thinking about visiting Salaam the next day. I almost didn't notice Udah walking toward me. As usual, she looked like a hippie in faded jeans, a gauzy white blouse, and flip-flops.

"I'm surprised to see you here," she said.

"Why's that?"

"Isn't it kind of late for you to be visiting?"

"I could ask you the same question, but I guess the better question for you is, 'Isn't it *too* late for you to be visiting?' Salaam is already asleep. You probably shouldn't disturb him. He looked very peaceful when I left him."

I intended to hurt and annoy Udah, and I knew that I was already violating a promise that I had just made to myself to change my ways. But I couldn't help myself. Udah seemed to be the only person who could come between me and Salaam. I had to let her know that would be a bad idea.

My words had the desired effect. She furrowed her brows and inhaled deeply. Then she pursed her lips in an obvious struggle to maintain her composure.

"Don't think that I believe for a second what you are implying. I know what you've been up to, and I know Salaam. He didn't make love to you tonight."

"You can delude yourself into believing whatever you want to believe. The truth is, he invited me to his apartment this evening, and when I went there, he greeted me with candlelight, flowers, and a beautiful satin robe. Then he gave me a wonderful massage with coconut oil." I raised the back of my hand to her face. "You can still smell it."

Udah pushed my hand away.

"Oh, I'm sorry," I said. "I guess you can still smell him on me as well."

"Look, your mind games won't work with me. I know your type. You're nothing but a shit load of trouble under a veneer of nail polish and lip gloss. Stay away from Salaam, and if you know what's good for you, you'll stay away from me as well."

I couldn't believe that she had the gall to talk to me this way.

"Let me tell you something, little girl. You know nothing about me and absolutely nothing about what I'm capable of. I'll squash you like an insect without a second thought. I've done worse without provocation. The only thing saving you now is the fact that we're standing in the middle of the lobby. You'd better not cross me again. You only get one warning."

Udah looked at me angrily, and then she smiled a strange smile.

"What the hell are you smiling about?"

"The irony of it all. You're only making it easier for me." She started swaying slightly and singing a Caribbean folk song softly under her breath. *"Pack she back to she Ma. Oh, pack she back to she Ma. A pretty little girl like Tessie Mahone. Pack she back to she Ma."* She hummed the rest of the tune as she turned around and left the building.

Her bizarre behavior unnerved me. I didn't know what to think about her, but I did know that she wasn't going to stop me from seeing

Salaam. At the same time, I realized that I would have to try harder to control my hostile impulses if I were going to turn my life around.

I returned home and went to bed hungry but determined to do better the next day. Maybe I would even apologize to Udah whenever I saw her again. That would certainly be a first!

Chapter 11

The next morning, I was awakened by hunger pangs. It had been a month since I had eaten, and my body was crying out for nourishment. I thought about the conversation that I had had with Salaam the night before and my run-in with Udah, and I still wanted to change my life. But who was I kidding? This was never going to work.

I sat up in bed and looked at the telephone that was on the nightstand. After a few minutes, I picked up the receiver and placed it in front of me, trying to decide whether to call Salaam. The clock caught my attention. It was 7:45, and Salaam was probably still at home. I dialed his number but hung up before his phone had a chance to ring.

What am I doing, I thought. *This doesn't make any kind of sense.*

I put the phone back on the nightstand, and it started to ring. I answered the call. It was Salaam.

"I'm sorry to call you so early, but I just wanted to make sure that you were all right before I go to work."

"Yes, I'm fine. I woke up a little while ago, and I've been thinking about our conversation last night."

"I've been thinking about it a lot, too. I meant what I said. I'll help you in any way that I can. You can call me at any time you need to. You have my cell phone number."

"Thank you. I'll give everything that happened last night some more thought. By the way," I added, "what does 'pack she back to she ma' mean?"

"It means, 'send her back to her mother.' It's from a song about a guy who's dissatisfied with his young wife because she's too lazy. What makes you ask a question like that?"

"It's just something I heard Udah singing. I ran into her last night when I was leaving your apartment."

"Oh." Salaam paused, probably trying to decide whether to open that can of worms. Opting to leave it alone, he said, "Well, I need to head out to work. Do you promise to call me if you need me?"

"I promise."

The next ten hours were miserable. I tried to take my mind off of my hunger by reading, but I couldn't concentrate. I took a long, hot bath, which usually would make me feel better, but I spent the whole time thinking about how satisfying it would be to consume some really intense necromantic energy, like Lynford's. I got out of the tub, put on my bathrobe, and went down to the kitchen. I don't really know why I did this, but I opened the refrigerator and looked inside. Of course, there was nothing in there for me. I went up to my bedroom to watch a movie. I couldn't focus on the story.

Finally, I gave in to my instincts. I went into my office and turned on my computer. *The Washington City Paper's* website was already bookmarked. On the events page, I discovered that there was a culinary arts convention going on at a hotel in Silver Spring. What a find – truly fertile hunting grounds!

What I needed was a good hunting outfit. I went to my bedroom where I selected a tight pencil skirt in a red knit fabric and a low-cut, cream colored sweater. There was a little voice in my head telling me to stop, but I chose to ignore it.

I put on a red lace thong and a pair of black stockings with red elastic lace at the top. The voice told me to reconsider what I was doing, but thinking was the last thing on my mind. I pulled the sweater over my head, covering my naked breasts, and stepped into the skirt. High heeled black ankle boots and a small black purse completed my outfit.

What are you doing? the voice asked.

"Shut up," I said aloud and descended the stairs.

I looked around in the living room for a few seconds and found my comb where I had left it, on the end table. I pulled most of my braids back and secured them with the silver comb, but I left some of the braids hanging free to frame my face.

Throwing a few essentials into my purse, I left my apartment to find a good meal.

The traffic on Rhode Island Avenue was unusually light, and I didn't see any taxicabs. I began walking the five or six blocks to Dupont Circle, expecting to catch a cab on the way, but none ever came.

No matter, I thought, *I can take the Metro.*

The ride from Dupont Circle to Silver Spring is a fairly long one. This gave me plenty of time to listen to the voice in my head, turn around, and go back home. Or I could have called Salaam. I had my cell phone with me, and his number was stored there. I could have gotten off the train at any number of stops and looked for something vegan to eat. I didn't think that would satisfy my hunger, but I could have at least tried it.

I didn't do any of these things.

I rode the train all the way to Silver Spring, sitting by the door so that I could sense the necromantic energy of each person that entered or exited near me. This fueled my appetite and strengthened my resolve. The little voice in my head was now silent. My foray into Salaam's world was apparently over, and I had reached my destination.

I briskly walked two blocks to the hotel and went downstairs to the ballroom where the convention was being held. Although it was scheduled to end in about an hour, there were still plenty of people milling about.

On display were all things culinary for residential and commercial kitchens: countertops and cabinets, major appliances, food processors and gadgets, cookware, bakeware, china sets, cutlery, and utensils. Everything and anything that a gourmet or gourmand could want was there. This type of gathering was sure to attract "foodies" reeking of necromantic energy.

At a booth promoting restaurant linens, I noticed a very tall, very overweight man who was deeply engrossed in examining napkins and tablecloths. He was well dressed, in a gray, glen plaid suit that appeared to be tailor made. His shoes were Italian, expensive, and well cared for. His skin was the color of butterscotch, his hair was closely cropped, and he sported a meticulously groomed beard and moustache.

I walked over to the booth and picked up a lacy tablecloth sample. "Ooh," I gushed, rubbing the fabric between my fingers. "This is really elegant!"

He glanced at me but immediately went back to what he was doing. Then something seemed to click in his mind, and he looked at me again. This time, I was able to catch his eye and enthrall him. He took a long look at me, dropped what he was doing, and walked over.

"That *is* beautiful, but here's something you should keep in mind. If you're purchasing this for a restaurant, it's going to be washed over and over again. That lace may not hold up well."

"That's a good point that I hadn't thought of. I guess it's obvious that I'm new to the business. I'm a great cook, and my dream is to open a restaurant, but I guess I've got a lot to learn."

"Oh, I'm sure you'll make your dream come true. With your style and beauty, anything is possible, as long as you have ambition, too."

"Thank you for your words of encouragement. Do you work in the restaurant business?"

"Yes."

He told me that his name was Brian. He owned two successful restaurants in Georgetown and Bethesda. He was in the process of opening another on the 14th and U Street corridor. I pretended to be interested and asked him countless questions as we walked around, exploring the items at the various exhibit booths throughout the hall. He seemed to be genuinely excited to share his knowledge and show off his business acumen. All the while, I stayed close to him, eventually even taking his arm, so that I could bask in the energy he was radiating. I was taking my time, making sure that I would be able to gain his trust and lure him into a private space where I could dine. I was too hungry to chance any mishaps.

Despite my friendly behavior towards him, he did not suggest that we hook up. We were already in a hotel, and I was sending strong signals, so it seemed that the logical thing for him to do was get us a room. He didn't, and I did not suggest it because I didn't want to scare him off.

Finally, someone made an announcement over the public address system indicating that the convention was closing for the evening. This presented me with the opportunity that I needed.

"Aw! I can't believe it's over already, and there's so much that I didn't get to see. Plus, I've really been enjoying your company and learning a lot from you, Brian."

"It's been a great time for me, too. Maybe we can exchange numbers and get together sometime for coffee or a meal. I could take you to one of my restaurants. I'd show you all the behind-the-scenes action that most people never get a chance to see."

"That would be wonderful! But what I'd really like to do right now, if it's possible, is check out your restaurant that's being reno-vated. I'd love to get a glimpse of the transformation of the space before it's complete. This might help me to understand what all would be involved in opening up my own place."

"Are you sure? It's already nine o'clock, so by the time we get there, it'll be pretty late."

"I don't mind that. I'm a night owl. Let's do it!"

"How can I resist you? Come on. I'll drive."

We made our way through the crowd to the hotel parking garage. Brian led me to his vehicle, which turned out to be a delivery van with the name of his restaurant, Carter's Café, emblazoned on the side.

"I'm sorry to take you in the company van, but I didn't expect to be driving a beautiful lady around this evening. The van is good, free advertising, so I use it most of the time instead of my BMW."

"You're just so full of tips! I'm learning so much just by being around you. I'm really glad that I decided to come to this convention."

On the way to his restaurant, Brian tried to make small talk by asking me questions about myself. I deftly avoided saying much of anything and instead kept the focus on him and his work. I was actually surprised at how interested he was in finding out about me. He didn't seem to be in any rush to get physical. Perhaps I had made a poor choice in targeting him.

"So tell me," I asked, "what is your favorite dish from the menu at your own restaurant?"

"Well, obviously, I enjoy eating. I like everything on the menu, but my favorite would have to be braised baby back ribs."

His café served Southern cuisine – smothered fried chicken, crab cakes, catfish, lamb chops – exactly the type of food that I wanted to hear about. I encouraged him to keep talking.

"Here we are," he finally announced, pulling the van into an alley and parking behind a rowhouse on U Street.

Ever the gentleman, he got out of the van and walked around to the passenger side to open the door for me. Graciously, he took my hand and helped me out.

"This is a great location and a beautiful building. I can't wait to see what you're doing to it on the inside."

"I hope you don't mind that we're going in through the back door."

"Of course not. In fact, it makes me feel like I'm part of the team."

Brian entered the building first and flipped the light switch. We were in the restaurant's large kitchen, which was almost completely finished being remodeled. The walls were painted bright white, and all of the appliances and countertops were made of stainless steel. The floors were covered in terra-cotta tile, and a combination of recessed lights and pendant fixtures illuminated the room.

"Those large boxes on the corner are filled with shelving and storage units that still need to be installed. I'm also bringing in a couple of movable islands to put in this large empty space in the middle of the room. That will expand the work surfaces."

"This is great! It's just how I would imagine your restaurant kitchen to look. What are in these boxes on the counter?" I asked, peeking into a box.

"Those are professional-grade cooking utensils – spatulas, whisks, and so forth."

"May I look at them?"

"Sure," he said, turning the box on its side and emptying out the contents.

"Very nice..."

"Let me show you the dining area."

We went through the swinging doors into the next room, and he turned on the lights. The room lacked furniture, but the walls had already been painted.

"I create an intimate dining atmosphere by keeping the general lighting low with wall sconces and placing votive candles on the tables. Also, texturing the walls with plaster and painting them in this dark brick color adds to the elegance of the dining room."

"I can picture what you're saying. It's going to be really beautiful. Can we go back into the kitchen? I want to check out your appliances and utensils again."

It was time for me to eat, and the kitchen was the best place for this meal. Once there, I walked over to the pile of utensils on the counter and picked up a barbecue fork.

"I'm surprised to see this here," I said matter-of-factly.

"My chefs don't use those a whole lot, but every once in a while, that's the only tool for the job."

"I see... That gives me an idea. Why don't you take off your jacket?"

"What for?"

"Just do as I say. Take off your jacket," I commanded. "Now, sit down on the floor."

He obeyed in silence and then looked up at me. The confusion and fear in his gentle eyes caused me to soften.

"I don't actually want to hurt you. You seem like a nice enough guy. But I have certain needs, and you can fulfill them."

"What are you talking about?" he whispered, his voice shaking.

"I need to eat, and you're edible. That's just how it is. For your sake, I wish there were another way."

"I'm edible?" he asked incredulously, eyeing the barbecue fork which was still in my hand.

"I know you're more than just food. You're also a person. And you're a businessman. You've got employees. I'm sure you've got friends, maybe a girlfriend or an ex-wife and a couple of kids. Your parents may still be alive, I don't know."

"They are! And I help to support them. They're elderly and don't have much income."

"I suppose your employees also depend on you for their livelihood, to take care of their own families."

"Yes, that's true! I'm important to a lot of people!"

"But what about me? I need you, too! Doesn't that matter? Don't I matter just as much as anyone else?"

"Yes, of course you do. I don't understand why you are turning against me. I was trying to help you. I was telling you anything that you wanted to know about opening a restaurant and making your dream come true. Isn't that what you wanted?"

"What are you talking about?! I'm talking about food. Eating to stay alive. I'm not trying to open a restaurant."

"I don't have any food here yet." He was trying to stand up but couldn't. "I can take you to one of my other restaurants, and you can have whatever you want."

"You don't serve what I need at your restaurant. I'm sorry, but this is just the way that it is."

I kneeled beside him and gently pushed him back. "Lie down, and it will all be over before you know it. Close your eyes."

Confused and unable to resist, he did as I said, reciting the Lord's Prayer under his breath. I turned his head away from me and pierced his jugular vein with the barbecue fork.

Despite my misgivings, I ate. I gulped down his blood, but I did not enjoy it. I blocked out any images of the sources of his necromantic energy as I consumed just enough to quell my hunger. I could not revel in the suffering of the animals that he had assimilated. And I could not pretend that Brian's life did not matter.

Though not fully satisfied, I stopped and stood up. There was Brian's lifeless body on the kitchen floor. Less than an hour ago, he was sharing his knowledge with me and treating me with respect and kindness. Now, he was just an inanimate thing composed of fat, muscle, bone, and skin. I had never really thought about this before. My actions had caused this being, a unique life, to vanish. I felt powerful, but it was a power that I never wanted to use again.

I covered Brian's head and upper body with his jacket and left the restaurant through the back door, determined not to cry this time. The U Street/Cardozo Metrorail station was only a block or two away, so I headed in that direction through the back alleys. I walked quickly with my head down, not wanting to see and not wanting to be seen. All I wanted was to get away from Brian's corpse and hide from myself. I wished that I could disappear.

Chapter 12

Taking the train home was a mistake. The 14th Street bus would have let me off less than half of a block from my building in a matter of maybe 15 minutes. Or I could have simply taken a taxi, and I would have been home in 10 minutes. But there was no direct route by train. I had to transfer from the Green Line to the Red Line in Chinatown, get off at the Dupont Circle station, and walk several blocks. I simply wasn't thinking straight.

During the entire trip, my mind kept going over and over what I had done, not just to Brian, but to so many men. I began to wonder if I were an abomination to feed on pain and death.

About a block from my building, my feet began to ache. I looked down at my boots and realized that I was wearing calfskin – the skin of a calf – as clothing without ever giving it a second thought. What was I doing? How could I be living this way? I must be a demon, and I wanted redemption.

I took off my boots right there in the street and threw them in the gutter. My purse was also made of leather, so I removed my keys and cell phone and tossed everything else down next to my boots.

I ran the rest of the way home in my stocking feet, but once I had entered the building's vestibule, I knew that I didn't want to go to my apartment. I didn't want to be by myself. Instead of going home, I went to the third floor and knocked on Salaam's door.

"Hi, Pearl! I was just..." He noticed my disheveled appearance. "What happened to you?"

I shook my head and said, "I don't even know if I can tell you. May I come in?"

"Of course!"

He opened the door wide so that I could pass, and he followed me in. As we walked down the stairs, he said to me, "Where are your shoes? Your foot is bleeding."

"I don't care. It doesn't matter."

"Of course it does. Sit down, and let me take care of it."

I dropped my keys and cell phone on the trunk and collapsed into the Papasan chair while Salaam went into the bathroom. Two-Faced approached me cautiously, sniffed the air around me, and then rubbed against my leg, while Twiggy jumped into my lap. I didn't feel like I had the energy to shoo them away, so I did nothing.

Salaam came back carrying a plastic tub of water. A towel was draped around his neck, and the pockets of his sweatpants bulged with supplies.

"Your stockings are ruined. Take them off, please."

"I can't. You do it."

"Okay, but don't get the wrong idea."

He put the tub of water on the floor beside the chair, and Twiggy jumped down to investigate. Salaam inched my skirt up, just high enough for him to access the top of my stockings.

Sensing his embarrassment, I looked away, and the Jamaican mask caught my eye. It was hideous, and I couldn't understand why Salaam kept it in such a prominent place, visible from practically every corner of his small apartment. I closed my eyes to avoid its lifeless stare.

Quickly, Salaam rolled each stocking down my leg and off of my foot.

"I'm going to wash your feet and put some antiseptic and a bandage on that cut of yours."

Once again, Salaam was caring for me through my feet. The water in the tub was warm and soothing as his hands soaped and rinsed my skin. He patted my feet dry, and with my eyes still closed, I could fully appreciate how soft the towel was. Then I felt him rubbing a slippery substance on the bottom of my left heel and covering it with an adhesive bandage.

"I hope that didn't hurt."

"No. It was nice."

I opened my eyes.

"Is the robe that you gave me still here? I'd like to get out of these clothes."

"Yes, I'll get it for you."

When he returned with the robe, I stood up and began to remove my skirt. Salaam averted his eyes.

"While you're changing, I'll put the towel and stuff in the bathroom," he said and left the room.

I had already put on the robe and was seated on the futon when Salaam came back. He sat down next to me and put his arm around me.

"Do you want to tell me what happened to your shoes?"

"In brief, I decided that I didn't want to have parts of a dead animal on my feet, so I threw them away."

"That's the last thing that I expected to hear you say! I think it's wonderful that you had such an epiphany, but you probably should've waited until you got home to go barefoot."

He hugged me and asked, "So what happened? Why the sudden, dramatic change of heart?"

"I was out doing the things that I normally do, and it just hit me that my life is empty. No one cares about me, and to tell you the truth, I don't really care about anyone else."

"Have you always felt this way?" He made himself comfortable in the seat, prepared to listen.

"Do you mean, have I always been so callous? It certainly seems that way, but that couldn't be true. I don't know. It's been such a long time since I've cared about anyone."

"Who was the last person you really loved?"

I put my head back and thought for more than a few minutes. Finally, I remembered a childhood friend, and the memories came flooding back.

"My best friend when I was a kid, Regina. We were always together and shared everything. Whenever either of us had a little money, we would go to the bakery around the corner from my house, buying as many gingerbread cookies as we could afford and splitting them equally between the two of us. We took a ballet class together for a while. I quit, but she stuck with it and became a pretty good dancer."

As I spoke, the years between then and now disappeared. I was a child again.

"Regina had a dog named Goldie who was hit by a car when we were about nine years old. I never particularly liked dogs, but Regina was devastated by Goldie's death, and I was devastated by Regina's grief. When we were a little older, we both had a crush on the same boy, but even this didn't divide us. Together, we wrote love notes to him which we intended to deliver at the same time. Our plan really didn't make much sense."

"But it's the way children think."

"Fortunately, we lost our nerve. We had so many adventures together over such a long period of time. Regina and I were inseparable until her family moved away."

"The two of you had a really special friendship."

"Yeah. I guess there was a time when I was able to love."

I needed to pour my heart out to someone, and Salaam was there. I began to express feelings to him that I hadn't even dared to admit to myself.

"Everything is different now. I'm alone. When I watch a great movie, I have no one to discuss its meaning with. When I listen to uplifting music, no one is there to experience its glory with me. When I read something profound, I can only repeat it to myself."

"That sounds very lonely."

"When I'm at home, I occasionally wonder how long it would take someone to find me if I fell down the stairs and was unable to reach the telephone. I always remind myself how farfetched this idea is. I'm strong and graceful. But still, if it happened, no one would miss me. Someone would find you in a minute."

As if to underscore how different Salaam's situation was from mine, his telephone rang.

"I don't have to get it," he suggested.

"No. Please go ahead and answer it. I'm glad that at least one of us has a connection to the world."

Salaam went to his desk to pick up his phone. Without much effort, I was able to hear the voice on the other end of the call.

"Hey Salaam, it's Lynford. If Pearl is with you, don't say my name."

"What's up?"

"Make up an excuse to leave the apartment now, and take your cell phone. I need to talk to you about something."

Salaam turned to me. "Pearl, I hope you don't mind if I take this call out into the hallway. I'll be as brief as I can."

"It's okay," I said. "Take your time."

Salaam left the apartment and walked a few yards down the hall. That wasn't far enough to prevent me from hearing both sides of his conversation. I stood by his front door and listened.

"So what's up?"

"You're not going to believe this! You remember that party I went to last week? And I told you that I saw Pearl leaving in a hurry?"

"Yeah. What about it?"

"Well, I just found out that Van was found dead up in one of the bedrooms. He had a vampire bite on his neck, and he bled to death. A couple of people said that they saw him heading upstairs with a woman who fits Pearl's description, and that was the last that anyone saw him alive."

Salaam took a deep breath.

"How do you know this is true?"

"Man, it's true! One of the people that saw them going upstairs was Clyde, and you know he's reliable. And I saw Pearl leaving the party myself, but I don't think that she saw me. I caught a glimpse of her through the window, and she looked pretty shaken up."

"All right. Don't worry about Pearl. I'm dealing with her now. I can help her turn this thing around."

"Is she there with you now? Brother, you need to stay away from her. That chick is crazy dangerous. I'll call the cops as soon as we hang up."

"You better not. I'm not kidding."

"What the hell is going on with you? What is it about you and that girl? She's making you blind, deaf, and stupid. You won't listen to reason. The things I'm telling you just go in one ear and out your ass."

"Look, you helped me do the wrong thing back in the day. Stay out of my way while I try to do right."

"If what I suspect is true, she's in an entirely different league. And you're not gonna rehabilitate her by feeding her vegetables or sexing her up."

"So you think the cops are gonna rehabilitate her? If what you say is true, think about it. Let's say she doesn't kill them, and they manage to arrest her and lock her up. Who does that benefit? The people who are dead are still dead. But she'd be suffering, too. It doesn't change anything for the better. It's nothing more than revenge. Isn't that why you never turned me in for what I did? If I can motivate her to change of her own free will and do something positive to make up for her past, things will be better than they are now."

"And if she kills someone else while you're 'rehabilitating' her?"

"She won't."

"I'm glad one of us is so confident about that. And what about Udah? I thought you wanted a vegan, tree-hugging woman. She's invested years of her life trying to get with you. Do you think she's gonna take this sitting down? Don't you know what she's capable of?"

"Udah *is* powerful, but there's nothing sinister about her. Her greatest power is her power of persuasion. And her compassion and patience. I've learned that first-hand, and I love her for it. But I think we both know that we'll never get together. After all the things that I've done... She deserves better; she just may not realize it yet."

"You're talking a lot of idealistic, philosophical mumbo jumbo. People's lives are at stake!"

"Look, I've tried to explain my reasoning to you. If you can't accept it, just butt out. None of this is your problem."

"Okay. I'm washing my hands of this whole mess. It's all on you now, my brother."

"That it is."

As Salaam walked back to his apartment, I returned to the futon. When he reentered the room, I wasn't sure what to expect, knowing what Lynford had told him. It seemed that he was on my side, but maybe it was just an act. I hoped I wouldn't have to defend myself against him. He wouldn't stand a chance.

He looked pensive as he descended the stairs.

"Anything wrong?" I asked.

"No. Nothing that I can't handle. I'm sorry about the interruption."

Salaam sat down on the futon next to me and sighed. Clearly, his heart was heavy.

"Maybe I should leave..."

"Please stay." He took my hand. "You want to feel connected to someone. I already feel a connection to you, and I suspect that it's actually mutual."

I pulled my hand away from him. "I really don't understand why you're being so good to me. Does your vegan code of ethics require it? I've done a lot of things that you would find reprehensible. If you only knew, you'd be running in the opposite direction."

"I can make the exact same statement about myself. You've got to realize that the past is immutable. There's nothing we can do about it. But it's also over and done with."

"The past may be over, but repercussions remain."

"To deal with them, we can only try to make the future better. You *will* make it better."

"How can you be so sure?"

"When I look at you, I see wonderful qualities that you probably don't even realize you possess."

"Like what? I suspect that you see the same things every other man sees: my body. Or do you have some special ability to perceive the imperceptible?"

He smiled.

"I don't know about that. But I do know that when I look at you with my third eye, I see inner beauty, artistry, vulnerability, and – most important – potential greatness. I see a person who longs to be loved and to love. I see someone who wants to do more than just survive day to day. I know that you're reaching for a higher purpose that you haven't found yet. I know you better than you realize because when I look at you, I see myself."

Listening to his words and looking into his eyes as he said them, I believed him, and I was relieved.

"I know exactly what you need," he said and stood up. "The Temptations' *Wings of Love* can cure anything."

He went over to the bookcase and selected an LP. The first song was a slow, romantic ballad.

"Come here."

Salaam took me by the hand and pulled me toward him. Reluctantly, I rose from the futon and placed my arms loosely around his neck. He put his hands on my waist and pulled me closer to him. I stood on my toes to avoid putting any pressure on my injured heel. This forced me to lean on him more than I had intended. He slid his hands down to my lower back and held me firmly to his body. As we slowly swayed together to the sound of the music, I rested my head on his chest. I could hear his heart beating, forcing life-sustaining blood through his arteries and veins. Blood that I didn't want to taste.

We danced this way without speaking for two or three songs, making slow revolutions in place.

Salaam was awakening my sensuality. It wasn't a burning lust, but an intense awareness of the parts of me that defined me as female, and an intense desire to be touched, caressed, and completed by him. I hadn't felt this way for such a long time. It was wonderful and frightening all at once. I had to pull away.

"Thank you for refreshing my dance skills," I said to break the spell, "but this is enough."

"Pearl, stop stopping yourself. Give yourself permission to enjoy life. If it's the last thing that I ever do, I'm going to give you one sensuous night when you allow yourself to feel unbridled pleasure."

"You're pretty ambitious, aren't you? And also a bit cocky."

"I'm glad to see that you're finally paying attention."

I smiled and shook my head.

"Now you sound like Lynford."

"Then I apologize. And I'd like to make an offering to you in exchange for your forgiveness. Why don't you have a seat over there," he said, gesturing towards the Papasan chair, "while I get it ready?"

I did as he requested, while he busied himself lowering the futon to the bed position.

"What are you doing?" I asked. "Are you expecting that sensuous night to be tonight?"

"I wouldn't be so presumptuous. This is just a preview. Trust me."

He went into the kitchenette and came back a little while later carrying a large plate with sliced strawberries, pineapple chunks, blueberries, almonds, and dark chocolate squares. He placed the plate in the middle of the bed.

"Please make yourself comfortable over here. I have one more thing to get."

He retrieved a bottle of wine, one wine glass, and a corkscrew from a cabinet. Once he joined me on the bed, we both sat cross-legged, facing each other, with the food and wine between us.

"Open your mouth."

He picked up a slice of strawberry with his fingers and placed it on my tongue. I moved the piece of fruit around in my mouth before I bit into it. It was sweet and tart and juicy. The flavor was familiar and pleasant.

"Again," he said, and I opened my mouth.

This time, he put in an almond and a piece of chocolate. I chewed them together. The combination was delicious. I had not remembered how wonderful simple foods like this tasted.

He went on feeding me this way until the plate was empty, eating only a few blueberries himself.

"I want you to try this wine. It's one of my favorites."

He uncorked the bottle and filled the glass almost to the top. I took a sip, and he told me to drink more. The wine was good, so I obeyed, drinking about one quarter of the contents. He took the glass from me and drank most of what remained.

"I know you're supposed to drink wine slowly, but I want to show you that I don't always do what I'm supposed to do. I've saved a little bit for you."

I took the glass from him, emptied it, and handed it back.

"Why don't you get under the covers while I move these things out of our way?"

He put everything on the trunk. I did not move. I just continued to sit there watching him as he pulled his T-shirt over his head, revealing his lean, muscular chest and arms. I couldn't stop staring at his chiseled abdominal muscles and well-developed pecs, punctuated by small black nipples. He turned off the lights, and I could hear rustling sounds as he removed his sweatpants.

"Come under the covers with me," he said as he climbed into the bed. I folded the bedspread back and got under. He moved close to me and reached for my waist in the darkness. Finding the belt of my robe, he undid the knot and slid the fabric off of my shoulders. Then he positioned himself on his back.

Lying close to him on my side, I rested my head on his shoulder and placed my hand on his chest. Encircling my body with the arm that was beneath me, he gently stroked my back with the tips of his fingers. I ran my hand down his smooth chest. His nipple grew hard under my touch, and I used my thumb to toy with it. His hand ventured past the waistband of my thong and gently caressed my hip.

Over the years, I had become expert in the art of seduction, but I hadn't been with a man whom I didn't intend to eat in such a long time that I wasn't confident about how to act. Yet, I was compelled by a force that seemed to be outside of me to slide my hand down his abdomen to the fabric of his shorts. I tried not to touch his private parts directly, but I couldn't help myself. My fingers were around him. However, the fabric of his boxers prevented my skin from touching his.

I placed my thigh on top of his. His thigh was now between mine. We rocked together in unison, Salaam moving in my hand, and my pelvis moving against his leg. My restless hand finally found its way into his boxer shorts through the leg opening.

"Not now," he whispered.

I pulled my hand back, embarrassed by the rejection. But he took my hand in his and held it to his chest. "It's okay," he said. "It's just not the right time, yet."

"Your body is telling me otherwise."

"Ignore it, and it will eventually quiet itself down."

Comforted but disappointed, I turned my back to him, and he pulled me close to his body. He put his arm over me and held my hand in his, up against my chest. He was warm, and I could feel that he was still hard and hear him breathing rapidly. Remembering what he looked like without a shirt – muscular chest, broad shoulders, strong arms, tight abdomen – I wished he would turn me around and make love to me.

He didn't. He just kissed me on my ear and whispered, "Good-night."

Chapter 13

The next morning, I was faced with the harsh reality of my situation. I needed to confess my murderous acts, but I could not. Living in Salaam's world was impossible, but going back to my own was no longer an option. I felt sick to my stomach and wanted to die.

Salaam was still sleeping peacefully. I rolled over on one side, resting my head on my hand, and looked at him lying there.

If it were not possible for me to live as a human with him, I thought, *perhaps I should make him like me. It would be so easy to start while he was asleep. And once the change was complete, he would accept his new life. Maybe he would even be grateful. I could offer him so much more than he had now, living in this tiny apartment and making practically no money working for his charitable organizations. With me, he could have anything that he wanted. Of course, he would have to give up being vegan.*

As if on cue, Salaam opened his eyes and looked at me. He smiled and caressed my cheek.

"Good morning, beautiful. How long have you been awake?"

"Not very long. Just long enough to watch you sleep and think about what I could do to you while you're lying there helpless."

"I hope it wouldn't be anything that I wouldn't enjoy."

I said nothing.

"Are you thinking about going home?"

"No. Not at all."

"Good. I was hoping you would say that. I'm going to make us a nice big breakfast, and I don't want to hear any protests against vegan food."

Salaam bounded out of bed and headed toward the large windows.

"Please don't open the blinds!"

"Are you sure you want to keep them closed? It's supposed to be a beautiful, sunny day today."

"I can't deal with the sunlight. Not right now."

"No problem. I'll get breakfast started."

Still wearing nothing but his boxers, Salaam went to the kitchenette and began pulling food out of the refrigerator, pans out of a lower cabinet, and utensils out of a drawer. The cats appeared and meowed for their food until Salaam filled their bowls. Soon, I could hear something sizzling and smell an aroma similar to bacon.

"What are you making?" I called out to him.

"Only good stuff. Five more minutes and you'll find out. If you want to go to the bathroom to freshen up, there's a new toothbrush in the medicine cabinet. You'll find it."

When I returned, Salaam had already put a fresh tablecloth, napkins, silverware, and salt and pepper shakers on the table. I sat down, and he placed a large plate of food at each place setting.

"What is all this stuff?"

"This is my special big breakfast. I only have it on weekends or holidays, when I know that I have time to be lazy. What we have here is tofu scrambled with onions, green peppers, and spices; hash browns; steamed asparagus; corn; and smoked tempeh strips, which are similar in taste to bacon. We've also got a couple of whole wheat bagels and vegan cream cheese. After we eat all of this, we'll probably need to go back to sleep. At least, I will."

"This is a lot. I doubt that I can eat this much."

"As long as you at least taste everything, I'll be happy. Dig in!"

I didn't want to eat this strange food. I wasn't sure how my body would react to it; it was so different from my usual diet. Nor did I want to offend or disappoint Salaam. As a happy medium, I tasted each item. Once again, I was pleasantly surprised. The food wasn't quite like the breakfast foods that I vaguely remembered, but it was good.

I managed to eat most of what he had served me. He cleaned his plate and ate my leftovers.

"I don't know about you, Pearl, but I'm just about ready to get back into bed and let my food digest. Did you like your breakfast?"

"I must admit, it was much better than I expected."

Salaam took me by the hand and led me back to the futon. We got under the covers, both lying face up. I had already discarded the thought of turning him. It was a stupid, desperate idea that clearly wouldn't fly. The idea of joining his world seemed a little more plausible.

"So how does someone become vegan anyway?"

"In essence, veganism is a state of mind. A person simply needs to make the decision not to use or consume any animal products – and then honor that decision. That's the difficult part. Some people jump in with both feet, immediately giving up all foods that are not plant based, throwing away any cosmetics or other items that have animal ingredients in them, and trashing or giving away clothing and furnishings made from leather, silk, wool, or fur. Other people take a more gradual approach. They may first stop eating red meat, then eliminate poultry and seafood from their diet. Eggs and dairy are usually the last to go because they're in so many baked goods. Afterwards, or at the same time, they deal with the issue of clothes, toiletries, and so forth."

"What did you do?"

"I jumped in head first. At the time, I had very few possessions, so it wasn't a big ordeal. You strike me as someone who would also do it all at once. Changing your diet would probably be relatively easy, given how empty your refrigerator is, but you have an apartment full of stuff that you would have to clear out, including some big-ticket leather items."

"Do you really think that becoming vegan would make my life better?"

"That depends on why you do it. If you do it because you've come to value and respect life and because you care about the planet, I believe that becoming vegan will move you to a new spiritual level. If you do it just to impress me or as part of a fad or because it's a good way to keep your weight under control, I don't think it will have the same impact on your spirit. But if you do it for any reason whatsoever, it will still benefit you, the animals, and the environment."

"I want to do it," I said softly, both to Salaam and myself. "I want to change my way of living and my way of thinking. I want to do something positive, for a change."

"I'll help you in any way that I can."

Salaam rolled over on his side and put his arm around me. We lay there together on the futon for a while, silently enjoying each other's company. Eventually, we drifted off to a restful sleep until there was a knock at the door. I immediately sensed that it was Lynford.

Salaam hastily put on his sweatpants.

"Hey, man," Lynford said when Salaam opened the door. "I just want to talk to you for a second."

"Go on."

"I guess I overstepped yesterday. Do your thing. I'll stay out of it, no hard feelings. You've changed a lot, and maybe there's something to your crazy new beliefs. I don't know, but you gotta do what you gotta do. I've got your back, whichever way you go."

"Thanks man. That's decent."

They clasped right hands and briefly embraced.

"So we're cool?" Salaam asked.

"We cool."

"I would invite you in, but I've got company already."

Acting as if that were an invitation, Lynford pushed past Salaam and walked to the top of the stairs. "Hi Pearl."

I looked up at him from under the covers and nodded my head.

"No need to get up," he said. "We're all friends here. I know you've missed me, but I can't stay. I've got places to do and things to be. You all will have to just keep on keepin' on without me."

"Very well then," I said. "Take care."

"Catch you later," he said to us both and left.

Salaam got back into the bed with me. He seemed ready to go back to sleep, but I wanted to talk. I knew that if I were to change my life, and include him in that new life, I would need to tell him the truth.

"Do you remember the conversation we had a while back – Lynford, Udah, you, and I – about the series of murders and whether the killer was a woman or a vampire?"

"Yeah." He turned onto his side to face me.

"Well, I was just thinking that there is really little difference between most people and vampires."

"That sounds a bit extreme. What do you mean?"

"It's like what we were all talking about before. A vampire kills people because she needs to eat them. Most people kill animals to eat them – they just do it at arms length, choosing to pay a middleman to do the dirty work. Humans view themselves as being at the top of the food chain – too bad for the lesser animals."

"I don't think that most people think about it that way. They probably don't think about it at all. In this country, people generally grow up eating meat. For the most part, they don't think of a piece of meat as being part of an animal. A lot of people have never even seen a live cow or chicken or pig. There's not really an intellectual – or maybe I should say an emotional – connection in their minds. Even among many animal lovers."

"Vampires must view themselves as being above humans on the food chain, the pinnacle of evolution," I said. "The daily activities, concerns, and dramas of human life are as insignificant to vampires as the day-to-day events in the life of a turkey are to humans. Does anybody really care whether Geoffrey the Gobbler got enough to eat today or was able to hook up with his mate?"

"I see your point. I really do, but I have to have faith that many people, once their eyes are open, will care about other animals, at least to the extent of trying to avoid complicity in their suffering."

I rolled onto my back and looked at the ceiling.

"You've been friends with Lynford for a long time. I'm sure you've shared all of your vegan information and philosophies with him, and he still hasn't changed. That doesn't support your theory."

"Maybe I just haven't found the right approach to reach him, yet."

"I've said it before, and I'll probably say it again. I don't understand why you are friends with him."

"Lynford is a good man. It's just hard to tell sometimes, through his jokes and crazy outfits."

"But he's not vegan."

"I don't believe that not being a vegan makes someone a bad person. You have to look at the totality of a person's value system to make any sort of assessment. And to do that, you really have to know them. And it's just not fair to judge a person's life before it is complete. I used to eat meat, and I've certainly made my share of mistakes, some with deadly consequences. I would be a hypocrite to reject him for doing what I've done and being where I've been. People develop and grow. People's experiences over time shape them, sometimes for the better, sometimes for the worse. Everyone messes up. If people are written off as a lost cause, there is no hope for the future. If people can't be forgiven and can't make amends, there's little motivation to change. If that's the case, we all lose. I don't want to believe that, and I want to work to make sure that it isn't the case."

"So you truly believe that no one is beyond forgiveness, beyond salvation?"

"As long as they're open to change, I believe that's true."

"What if we're not talking about a person who feeds on animals, but about an actual vampire who feeds on humans?"

"Well, logically, the same principles apply. Humans are animals, just a type of animal that isn't usually used for food."

"What if the murders we were talking about really were incidences of a vampire slaughtering men for food?"

"That's just the same question asked a different way. The answer is still the same. What do you really want to ask?"

I paused, wondering whether I should reveal my secret to Salaam. I turned to face him.

"Remember when Udah said that Lynford had turned his body into a graveyard by eating carcasses? Well, I'm a grave robber."

"What does that mean?"

"When a person eats butchered animals, negative energy is also consumed and enters the person's bloodstream. Someone who feeds on necromantic energy in blood could be considered a grave robber."

"Okay, I'll buy that. But what does that have to do with you?"

I was surprised at how calm and open-minded Salaam was. This gave me the courage to go on and answer his question honestly.

"Those men were killed by someone feeding on the necromantic energy in their blood – a vampire."

"And how do you know this?"

"What if I told you that I'm the vampire who killed them?"

"I would ask you to stop killing," he said, continuing to speak in an unemotional voice.

"I don't know if I can." I placed my hand over my face and began to cry. Salaam tried to hold me, but I pulled away from him. "You don't seem terribly shocked. Don't you believe me?"

"I believe you, but I also believe that you want to change the path that you've been on. I could sense that from the moment that we first spoke, even if you weren't aware of it yet."

"If I had known what I would become, I would have never started down the path that has led me to where I am now."

"What happened? I mean, how did this all start?"

I took a deep breath to calm myself, and then I sat up and told Salaam my story. He listened intently, without interruption.

"After I graduated from college, I got a corporate job that paid well, but I quickly grew tired of the monotonous routine. I decided that it would be much easier and more interesting to find a man of means who would take care of me. I was young, smart, and good-looking. How difficult would it be?

"I did all of the usual things to find a good candidate: business functions, happy hours at upscale bars, gallery openings, dinner parties at well-connected friends' homes, and so forth.

"I dated plenty of men, but none of them met my criteria until I met Kwamena. I was at an exclusive nightclub with a couple of my girlfriends, drinking, dancing, and checking people out. I'll never forget it. I was wearing an elegant purple cocktail dress and a pair of silver sandals.

"I spotted Kwamena, a handsome, dark-skinned man, standing at the bar, waiting to buy a drink. He was wearing a very expensive, well-fitting suit. I placed my drink at an empty table and went to the bar to order a fresh one. Standing next to Kwamena, I noticed that he had a large but tasteful diamond ring on his right hand, along with a Rolex on his left wrist. I waited for him to smile at me. If he had good teeth, I thought, he might just be the man I was looking for. He flashed a million-dollar smile at me, offered me a top-shelf brandy, and I was hooked.

"That night, he gave me a ride home in his Mercedes-Benz. Later that week, he took me to dinner at an expensive French restaurant. The following weekend, he took me to his place to watch a movie. His 'place' was a mansion in Potomac, and we watched a movie in his media room, which was more like a professional screening room, including stadium seating for a dozen people and the biggest screen that I had ever seen in someone's home.

"Up until this point, he had behaved as a perfect gentleman. But when it was time for me to leave and we were saying goodbye, he kissed me passionately on the lips and all over my face. I was a bit surprised, but I went along with it. Then his hands went around my neck, and without warning, he pierced my neck with something sharp on his ring. His kisses moved from my face to my neck, and I felt a sucking sensation. I tried to push him away from me, but he held me too tightly. He continued to suck on my neck as I struggled against him. Finally, he let me go.

"He apologized, claiming that he had simply gotten carried away. Then he took me to his bathroom, where he cleaned my wound and covered it with a bandage. Afterwards, he drove me home, chatting as though nothing had happened, and promised to call me the next day.

"He did in fact call me, and blinded by his wealth, I agreed to go out with him again in a few days. He took me to a nighttime baseball game and back to his home. This time, we ended up in his enormous and incredibly beautiful bedroom. We made love between his silk sheets. I thought we were done, but he moved down beneath the covers and began kissing my belly. As he moved lower, I expected him to pleasure me with his tongue, but instead, I felt a sharp jab near the top of my inner thigh. Again, his lips covered the wound, and he sucked my blood. I tried to push his head back, but his grip was strong, and he stopped only when he had had enough. This time, he didn't apologize. He simply behaved as though nothing unusual had happened.

"I told myself that I would never see that lunatic again. I stopped taking his calls and tried to forget about him. Unfortunately, I could not get him out of my mind. He had enthralled me. The more time passed, the less I thought about his strange behavior, and the more I thought about sharing his wealth with him. I finally took his call and agreed to meet him at his place one evening.

"It was just after sunset, and he brought me out back to his swimming pool. He had a lovely selection of *hors d'oeuvres* and a bottle of champagne nicely arranged on the table. Sitting there in that beautiful environment, he told me that I, too, could be just as wealthy as he was, and he could show me how, if I would let him. He explained to me the whole thing about necromantic energy. He said that drinking human blood had made him powerful beyond what was considered natural. That was why most cultures frowned upon cannibalism. He was more than human, and if I would allow him to drink my blood one more time, not only would he be strengthened, but I would become like him. If I didn't allow him to taste me again, he would drain my blood, and I would die. Either way, he would win. If I chose to cooperate, we would both win.

"There wasn't much that I could do, but to be honest, I was still looking for a shortcut to easy street, so I would have agreed even without the threat.

"He took my hand, turned my wrist upright, and sliced into it with his ring. Blood began to flow from my wound, and he lapped it up from my hand and arm before covering the incision with his mouth. I swear that I could feel the change within me almost immediately.

"We spent the next several hours together. During that time, he taught me the traditions that had worked so well for so long – avoiding sunlight and mirrors, waiting for an invitation to enter his prey's home, sexually arousing his prey before the kill. He explained that I would have enhanced mental powers and a greater ability to perceive. He advised me to completely consume my prey, and to avoid turning anyone unless I was positive that they could be trusted. He told me that he wanted to move me into his home so that we could hunt together as well as feed off of each other, which was something that he found to be extremely erotic. He admitted that he was lonely, his footsteps echoing in the huge, empty rooms of his home.

"I told him that I wanted to be with him, too. Soon afterwards, I drove away from his home, never to return.

"From that point on, I've lived on a diet of human blood. My material wealth has increased substantially year after year while the amount of work that I actually perform has decreased proportionately.

It sounds like a blessing, but in reality, it has been a curse. I am lonely beyond belief, usually bored, and I can't stand myself."

Tears began to flow freely from my eyes again. This time, I let Salaam hold me.

Salaam finally spoke. "I can and will help you change; you've just got to trust in me. You've got to stop your destructive behavior in order to heal yourself. Please let me help you."

"I don't know if I can survive without consuming necromantic energy so I continue to hunt. But I'm not even sure that I want to live. I don't know why I go on this way. I'm cursed."

"All the more reason for you to let me help you. I'll show you another way to live. Things can't get any worse..."

"I guess you're right. I'm going to go home now and pull myself together. Then I'll work on a plan to get the change started. I'll call you for your help. I know I'll need it, and I know that I can trust you."

"Are you sure you should be alone right now?"

"Yes, I'll be fine. I already feel like a burden has been lifted."

Salaam kissed me on the forehead before releasing me.

I got dressed and returned to my apartment, determined to adopt a new way of life.

Chapter 14

Unfortunately, the last words that I had said to Salaam were lies. I wasn't fine, and I didn't call on him for help. In fact, I completely avoided him, convinced that I could make the change on my own. I refused to answer his phone calls or to go to the door when he knocked.

For about two weeks, I tried living on salads and fruit. I drank huge quantities of water, juice, and herbal tea. As a result, I was hungry all the time and making frequent trips to the bathroom to rid my body of all of the extra fluid I had been consuming.

If this is what it's like to be vegan, I thought, *I'd be better off remaining a vampire!*

In moments of weakness, I got on the Internet and searched for opportunities to hunt. I found many, and even got dressed for the kill a few times, but I never actually made it out of the apartment.

In a move that was completely foreign to me, I visited websites that featured pictures of "beautiful men." I fantasized about some of them – what they had eaten and how I would eat them. Just as I was sitting at my desk, imagining myself sucking the life out of a particularly muscular man, my train of thought was broken by the sound of loud, rapid knocking at my front door. Even when I was almost at the door, I couldn't sense any necromantic energy.

It's Salaam, I thought.

I was finally ready to admit that I needed his help, but when I opened the door, Udah was standing there, in all of her neo-hippy, karma-free glory. I guess she never tired of jeans, flip-flops, and wispy blouses.

"You're the last person I expected or wanted to see."

"Look, I know that our most recent encounter was pretty ugly, and I'm sorry for that. But I really need to speak to you. Can we put that behind us for just a few minutes?"

"Sure!" I said sarcastically. "Why not? Come on in, and make yourself at home."

Udah brushed past me and climbed the stairs into my apartment. She strolled over to my piano and slid her hand across the high-gloss surface. My comb was on top of it, but Udah seemed to ignore it. Standing there with raised eyebrows, she slowly looked around the room, judging it – judging me – like an uptight schoolmarm.

"This is impressive," she finally said.

"Yes, it is. What do you want?"

"I want to talk to you about Salaam."

"What a surprise."

"I know that you've been seeing each other and that you even slept with him."

"Now, I really am surprised. Salaam doesn't seem the type to kiss and tell." I thought for a moment. "Lynford, on the other hand..."

"It doesn't really matter how I found out. The point is, Salaam takes intimacy very seriously, more seriously than most men. He wouldn't have spent the night with you if he didn't have strong feelings for you."

"Well, I'm glad that you're finally facing reality."

"Reality is no stranger to me. I've been hip to the real you since day one. So has Salaam. He and I share a lot of things in common, including the desire to 'save the world.' The difference is, I can recognize a lost cause, and he can't."

Udah looked at the piano again, and this time, my comb caught her attention. She picked it up and began to examine it.

"Are you trying to equate me with a lost cause?"

"Poor choice of words. Sorry."

"Not a very convincing apology. Just get to the point and get out."

"Look, you've got to understand that Salaam was in a really bad place not all that long ago, in the grand scheme of things. It took a tragedy and a lot of work for him to turn himself around. If you care for him, you won't make him go back there."

"First of all, I'm not 'making him' do anything. And you've got a hell of a lot of nerve to imply that I'm some type of evil influence."

"Pearl, I know what you are. Do I have to spell it out?"

Udah had chosen the wrong time to come and confront me. I was in no mood to listen to anything that she might have to say. However, I was in the mood to put her out of my misery.

I walked over to where she was standing and snatched my comb away from her. Then I grabbed her by the throat with one hand, forcing her back against the wall.

"I warned you to stay out of my way before, and I told you that I wouldn't warn you again."

Udah pulled at my hand with both of hers, to no avail.

"I know you're trying to change, Pearl," she was barely able to whisper.

I loosened my grip so she could speak but didn't let go. She would surely change her tune. I hoped she would beg for her life.

"But what you're doing right now proves my point."

"So why should I stop? It would be a shame to disappoint you, prove you wrong."

"Do it for yourself and for Salaam."

I ignored her words.

"You're hardly worth the effort, a one-calorie kill, so to speak, but I'd get a lot of satisfaction from closing your trap for good."

I slowly tightened my grip around her throat. I wanted to take out all of my frustration on her. I wanted to see her suffer, as much as I was suffering. She struggled but was no match for me. I looked in her eyes and saw my own pain and fear reflected back at me. I thought about my torment and the promises that I had made to Salaam and to myself to change my life for the better. I began to regret what I was doing, but how could I stop now? This had already gone too far.

As she was beginning to lose consciousness, I heard a knock at my door again. In my agitated state, I panicked and assumed it was Salaam. I needed a moment to decide what to do. I let go of Udah, and she slid down the wall to the floor, coughing and rubbing her throat.

I heard knocking again, this time louder and faster.

"Pearl," Lynford shouted. "I know you're in there, and I know that Udah is with you. Open the door!"

Reluctantly, I let him in without saying a word.

"Where's Udah?" he said as he bounded up the stairs, three at a time. I followed him, walking slowly. When he reached the landing, he found Udah sitting on the floor, leaning against the wall and rubbing her throat.

"What have you done to her?" He took Udah's chin in his hand and turned her head from one side to the other, looking at her neck.

"As you can see," I whispered, "I haven't done anything to her, at least nothing that she won't recover from."

He flashed an exasperated look at me.

"Udah, are you okay? Say something."

She stuttered in a hoarse voice, "I... I'm okay. She can't really hurt me."

"Come on," he said, helping Udah to her feet. "Let's get out of here."

Even after they left, I didn't know what to do. I paced back and forth in my living room. My first thought was to turn to Salaam for support, but he would be outraged by what I had almost done to Udah. Anyway, Lynford and Udah probably went straight to his apartment to tell him everything. Maybe he wasn't home. That would give me more time to think. Maybe I should go out somewhere.

Before I could come up with a plan, I heard knocking at my door yet again. At this point, it could only be one person. I let Salaam in.

He looked at me with quiet anger as he entered my apartment. Embarrassed and ashamed, I averted my eyes and turned around to slowly close the door. I tried to think of something clever to say, but nothing came to mind. We climbed the stairs in silence. Once in the living room, he pulled the bench out from beneath the piano and sat down, facing the sofa.

"What happened here?"

Feeling like a juvenile delinquent who had just been called into the principal's office, I sat on the arm of the couch nearest Salaam. It was an awkward, uncomfortable position, both literally and figuratively, but it made me feel like I could get up and bolt easily at any time.

Salaam just sat there staring at me. I looked at the floor. Eventually, the silence became more difficult to bear than any conversation would have been, so I spoke.

"I'm not a monster."

"No, but you're acting like one," he said angrily. "What happened? Why'd you attack Udah, and why didn't you accept the support that I offered you before things got to this point?"

"I was trying to become vegan, and I was trying to do it on my own. I really wanted to change, but I guess I thought it would be a lot easier than it actually was."

Salaam continued to look at me without speaking, so I babbled on.

"Truth be told, I was hungry and irritable, and Udah came by at just the wrong time. But she's okay. Really."

Salaam still wouldn't speak.

"Things are actually different for me. I regretted what I was doing pretty much as soon as the altercation started – I just didn't know how to stop."

Finally, Salaam responded.

"I would gladly offer myself to you to ease your struggle," he said in a quiet voice, "but I don't have the necromantic energy that you crave. Anyway, that wouldn't help you to change. What you really need is specific advice, especially on how to select foods that will make you feel full and satisfied – that will take away your hunger and cravings. I bet you were trying to live on lettuce and tomatoes. That's what people always do, and it never works!"

His words angered me. As if it were so simple!

"You have no idea what I'm even talking about! It's not just about nutrition or the right foods. There's so much more to it!" I needed to be heard and understood. "I'm accustomed to the excitement of choosing the perfect outfit in anticipation of the hunt. The exhilaration of finding a fertile, new hunting ground. The suspense of pursuing a specific man, and the thrill of capturing him. The ecstasy that takes over my body as I feel his warm blood filling my mouth, coursing down my throat, energizing my body, and satisfying me – both physically and emotionally."

"You think that I can't understand that?" he said calmly. "I understand completely. Consuming a person's necromantic energy is more than delicious. It's a rush and a high that's almost orgasmic. No, it's better than an orgasm because it lasts longer. And when you're finished, and your prey is lying there wilted and empty, you have an overwhelming feeling of power that can last for weeks. I know the feeling well. I indulged in it as often as I could for years before I became vegan."

I was stunned. "How can that be?"

"I became a vampire as a teenager. I already told you how I got involved in the drug economy. At the time, I wasn't amoral. I was trying to help my family; I didn't have a lot of options; and I thought that selling drugs was a victimless crime. After all, nobody was forcing people to use, and how users got their money was beyond my control. I didn't understand the big picture. I just knew that I needed to make some money, and I did everything possible to make plenty of it. And I was highly successful.

"Unfortunately, my success did not go unnoticed. One day, my supplier brought me to meet Holden, the guy who controlled the drug trade in most of the city. We met at night at his mansion. I was brought into his office, where he sat behind a massive desk. As I stood in front of him, he said that he would grant me unimaginable power and wealth if I had the balls to cross over into an entirely new existence. I told him that I was afraid of nothing.

"He told me that he was a vampire and was going to share that gift with me. I was surprised and more than a little skeptical, but I said nothing. From one of the lower desk drawers, he removed a small wooden box and placed it in the middle of the desk. He flipped the cover open, and I could see that the box contained a length of rubber tubing, a packet of bandages, and an awl."

"What's an 'awl'?" I asked.

"It's a carpentry tool, a pointed piece of metal with a handle used to poke small holes into wood or leather."

Salaam continued with his story.

"Holden told me to grab a chair and pull it over to the side of his desk. I did so and sat down. He tied the rubber tubing tightly around my upper arm and tapped my inner elbow several times with his first two fingers to make a blood vessel rise to the surface. I was scared of what he was going to do, but even more afraid of what he might do if I showed my fear. So I remained stoic.

"He removed the awl from the box with one hand, held my arm tightly with the other, and pierced the vein in my arm. I was horrified as he placed his mouth on my arm and began to drink my blood. Eventually, he took a bandage from the box and told me to press it against the wound. He said that one of his men would show me to a room where I could rest, and that he would repeat this process twice more in order to turn me.

"I spent the next few weeks as a reluctant guest at his home. Most of the time, I was alone in the room that he provided to me. Every few days, he would stop by to instruct me on how I was to behave after the change was complete. He told me to shun sunlight and remain secretive and solitary. He said that the need for companionship is a weakness, that compassion is a weakness. He told me that vampires are the master race and have the right to dominate all other beings. It was our destiny to consume those below us, distilling and concentrating their life forces into our own. This would maintain our status on top.

"After about two weeks of my imprisonment, Holden again drank my blood. After about four weeks, one of his henchmen brought me to his office where he drank my blood for the third and final time. I immediately felt a change come over me, just as you described. My fear and apprehension transformed into a feeling of omnipotence.

"Holden said to a couple of his henchmen, 'Bring her in.' They left the room and came back immediately with a teenage girl – very beautiful, plump, and dressed in something tight and revealing, with a low neckline. As the henchmen left, Holden called the girl forward. She stood before him, crying as he picked up a paring knife that was on the desk and absentmindedly twirled and flipped it between his fingers.

"He told me that I was going to drink the girl's blood, and as I did, I would absorb the necromantic energy that she had accumulated from every creature that she had consumed over the course of her lifetime. This dark energy would imbue me with mystical powers of perception. He said that I would be able to control the actions of others. That women would find me irresistible. That men would respect and worship me. He claimed that I would live forever and never get older.

"Holden ordered the girl to come closer to him, and as if in a trance, she obeyed. He held her by the chin, tilted her head to the side, and made a short incision in the side of her throat. Roughly, he pushed the girl over to me and said, 'Drink.' I hesitated for only a few seconds before I began to suck and lap up the blood greedily. I was hungry for even more power.

"The girl tried to fight me, but she wasn't able to free herself, and I drained her completely. Her limp body collapsed onto the floor.

"After that, I became more powerful and more ruthless. At first, I would pick up women at bars and nightclubs and consume them. I used the Afro pick that I told you about as my utensil of choice. After a while, I stopped hunting. Instead, I would send one of my men out to find me women to eat. I called them 'fast food,' and I didn't care how he got them, as long as they were clean and healthy.

"My mother's death finally opened my eyes to what I had become. I locked myself away for a couple of months to grieve. Then I burned the pick and packed just a few of my things in a small knapsack and left town. Somehow, I found my way to Washington, DC, and I met Udah. Although I didn't know how veganism would affect me as a vampire, I knew that I had to turn myself completely around.

"That was when I discovered that vampires don't actually need necromantic energy to survive. I realized that it's not a nutrient. It's an addictive substance. And vampirism is learned behavior, a practice that has been passed down for centuries. It's about what you do, not who you are.

"Necromantic energy builds up inside of you, depleting your humanity, and you forget how to love, care, be tender. Continuing to consume necromantic energy is what traps you in the form of a vampire. But you can return to normal; all you have to do is stop. Once I became vegan, I became human again.

"Living as a vampire is a choice. You may not realize that the choice is there, but it is. And now that you know that you have a choice, what will you do?"

Without hesitation, I responded, "I want to change, but it's too hard! I really have been trying..."

"Giving up necromantic energy can be like giving up a narcotic. But it gets easier over time."

"Do you still crave it?"

"At first, I did. But not anymore. In due time, the idea of drinking blood will become disgusting to you. Once you become a vegan, your spirit will no longer be bogged down by your own appetite. Living well does not revolve around eating badly."

Salaam's words resonated with me, and I finally truly understood that I could change what I was. And I didn't have to be alone in my transition. Salaam could help me, and I would accept his support.

"Salaam, I'm ready. I see clearly now, and I'm turning to you for guidance."

I looked around the room and found my comb on the floor.

"Please take this and destroy it. I don't want it anymore."

Salaam let out a huge sigh of relief as he took the comb from me. Then we embraced.

"We'll get started first thing tomorrow, so get some good rest tonight. I'm going to give Udah a call to make sure she's all right." He smiled. "I'm proud of you."

As soon as Salaam left, I went to bed, although it was still very early, to think about everything that had happened and everything that Salaam had shared with me. Tomorrow would be a new day.

Chapter 15

That night, once I was finally able to fall asleep, I was tormented by dreams of the men that I had eaten, particularly those whom I had killed since the time that I had met Salaam and was first introduced to the idea of veganism. Images of their dead faces haunted me – the stillness, the slackness, the blankness.

I also dreamed about the people that they had left behind, my mind inventing personas for persons whom I had never met: Jean, the girlfriend of the man I killed at the party; Brian's employees at his two restaurants; Tom's sickly son and widow; Lisa, the girl that Tony dropped for me at the seafood restaurant; Ben's celebrity friends; and the many aunts and uncles and nieces and nephews of Jesus and Arturo.

All of the hurt, loneliness, and grief that they suffered was because of me, because of my appetite. What was I, to be able to cause so much pain, suffering, and death? I didn't want to be this anymore.

I was relieved to be awakened by the sound of my telephone ringing.

"Good morning," Salaam said when I answered the phone. "I hope you're well rested."

"I didn't sleep well, but I'll be fine."

"Okay. We have a lot to get done today, and it's already almost eleven o'clock. I'm coming over in about an hour to show you what you need to do. Get dressed in something comfortable, and be ready to spend the entire day with me."

Normally, I bristled at the idea of anyone giving me orders. In this instance, I was more than happy to be compliant. "I'll be ready and waiting."

As soon as I hung up the phone, I got out of bed and went into the bathroom to wash up. While the water was running for my bath, I looked down at my body. I had always had a sexy, curvaceous figure, but since I had become a vampire, my body had become even more voluptuous. I had used my body as a tool – a weapon – to lure my victims. I wondered if becoming vegan would change the way that I looked and make me less sexy. *That might actually be a good thing*, I thought. I wanted to look at my face in the mirror, but I couldn't. *That might be a good thing as well.*

I took my bath and dressed myself in a pair of black yoga pants and a tan, cotton tunic. The long, loose top concealed my curves and seemed appropriate for the task ahead. It was the exact opposite of a hunting outfit.

At about noon, Salaam showed up looking more businesslike than usual in a buttoned-down shirt and khaki pants. He had a large canvas bag hanging from his shoulder and a tray in his hands.

"I know that you don't keep much of anything in your refrigerator, so I brought brunch for both of us."

"What do you need me to do?"

"You can set the table while I lay out our spread."

Salaam removed from the tray a plate of whole-grain pancakes covered in foil, a container of minced yellow squash with onions and tofu, and a bowl of steamed spinach. In the canvas bag, he had a small bottle of maple syrup, a bag of sliced fresh fruit, a carton of soy milk, and a box of Chai green tea bags. Last, he removed a plastic container of cookies.

"Are those –?" I took the lid off of the container and inhaled the familiar, spicy aroma.

"Yes. Vegan gingerbread cookies."

I was touched that he remembered my childhood treat. I couldn't think of anyone who had cared enough to really listen to me and try to surprise me with a simple, thoughtful gesture – their only goal to make me happy. I wasn't sure how to respond, so I just smiled at Salaam and ate one of the cookies. It was delicious!

"Okay," he said. "Today is day one of vegan boot camp. You're going to eat a nice big meal while I teach you the basics of nutrition."

While we ate together at the dining room table, Salaam lectured me on the vegan diet. He told me that I should think about nutrition in terms of the four food groups: fruits, beans and legumes, whole grains, and vegetables. My diet should revolve around complex carbohydrates and fiber so that I would feel full. I should also include a wide variety of colorful fruits and vegetables to get plenty of vitamins and antioxidants.

I listened carefully and took mental notes. But at the same time, I couldn't stop myself from thinking about how much I would like to spend every day with Salaam. He was intelligent, kind, and attractive – probably better than what I deserved, but he was what I wanted.

Once we had finished eating and had put the dishes and empty containers in the dishwasher, he grabbed the canvas bag and sat down with me on the sofa. I hoped that we would relax and have a casual conversation, but he was focused on one thing only: my transformation.

"This is homework for you to read after I'm gone this evening." He pulled out a stack of papers, books, and pamphlets.

"First of all, 'Vegetarian Starter Kits' from the Physicians Committee for Responsible Medicine and PETA. And you've got to read, *By Any Greens Necessary: A Revolutionary Guide for Black Women Who Want to Eat Great, Get Healthy, Lose Weight, and Look Phat* by Tracye McQuirter. Compassion Over Killing's 'Veg-DC Dining Guide' is for you to use when you're away from home. This pamphlet is the Vegetarian Resource Group's reference list of food ingredients. It explains what they're actually made of and whether they're vegan. When you go shopping, you need to read the labels of prepared foods carefully to make sure that they don't contain anything that you don't want to eat. I also brought a nutrition DVD by Dr. Michael Greger for you to watch. And here's a list of vegan resources on the Internet. Check them out this week."

"I never realized there was so much to learn..."

"And a lot to unlearn. You need some basic knowledge about nutrition that's not put out by people trying to sell you stuff that's going to kill you. All of the groups I'm referring you to are nonprofit organizations."

He gave me a pad and pen from his bag.

"Now let's make a shopping list. We should get some whole-grain pasta, brown rice, dried beans, spices, and vegan multivitamins. These items will last a long time, so we can buy large quantities. You'll also need pasta sauce, peanut butter, cold cereal, rice or soy milk, oatmeal, and tofu in those little aseptic boxes. These items also store pretty well, so we can get plenty. Next, we'll get you some yams, apples and citrus fruit, onions, garlic –"

"Garlic?"

"Yes, garlic. You're not a vampire anymore. You can and should eat plenty of garlic. It's good for you!"

"I hope you don't envision long garlic garlands draped throughout my kitchen. I don't think I could take that."

Salaam smiled and squeezed my knee. Finally, I had gotten him to pause for a minute and lighten up.

"I'm glad that you can see some humor in this. I was afraid that I might be boring you with too many facts and instructions."

"No. This is exactly what I need."

"So, where was I? Oh, yeah. Next, the perishable stuff that you'll need to buy fresh once or twice a week. I'm talking about whole-grain bread, kale, collard greens, tomatoes, bell peppers, celery, asparagus, squash, sprouts, romaine lettuce, and seasonal fruits and berries. Buy organic and locally grown whenever you can."

"Why?"

"Locally grown to support local farms and to protect the environment by reducing the need to ship produce long distances. I'm assuming that you're interested in protecting the environment..."

"I hadn't really thought much about it, but I guess it goes hand in hand with being vegan."

"It does! Most people don't know that animal agriculture causes more greenhouse gas emissions than all forms of transportation combined! It's in a United Nations' report. Switching to a vegan diet does more for the environment than switching to a hybrid car. It also conserves water, reduces pollution from farmed animal waste, and eliminates the need to cut down forests to create grazing land for cattle."

"Really! What about buying organic? Why do that?"

"Buying organic foods means that you won't end up eating pesticides. And as the demand for organic produce goes up, there'll be an overall reduction in the use of these chemicals, which end up becoming pollution."

"Okay. Back to our grocery list. Do I need special appliances to cook the foods that you're suggesting?"

"No. All of these foods can be prepared with your basic, regular cookware. But if you like to cook and you want to get fancy, we can get you some vegan cookbooks, a blender, a food processor, and a juicer."

"I did like to cook a long time ago, but let's take it one step at a time. This is already a bit overwhelming."

"Don't worry. I plan to be with you every day for the next three weeks to make sure that you're on track and to help you if you stumble. It takes about 21 days for your taste buds to change and become accustomed to a vegan diet. Until then, I'll be here to hold your hand."

"I hope you mean that literally."

He took my hand and pressed it to his lips. "I do."

We spent the rest of the day talking about nutrition, dishes that I might enjoy eating, restaurants to check out, and health food stores that were nearby. Once the sun went down, we went shopping, first to buy all of the kitchenware that I lacked and then to buy the items on the grocery list that we had developed together earlier in the day. By the time that we returned home and put everything away, I was exhausted and famished.

But Salaam would not let up. He showed me how, in only about 20 minutes, I could prepare a filling meal of wholewheat spaghetti smothered in tomato sauce with chunks of eggplant, onion, mushrooms, and green peppers. After we ate together, he went home, and I went to bed.

The next day, and every day thereafter for the next three weeks, he came over to my apartment in the early afternoon, or I went to his place after he returned home from work. He told me that he had rearranged his work schedule so that he could focus on me. Each day, we cooked and ate at least two meals together. Each day, my attraction to him grew stronger.

Our time together didn't focus solely on food. We also spent time talking about compassion and the purpose of life. He encouraged me to be more selective about what I read and watched, focusing more on media with a positive message – or at least some type of insight – and less on pointless violence. He had me watch *Groundhog Day* with him, a movie that he said should be required viewing for everyone, not for its humor but for its message about how to live a fulfilling life. We also watched *The Witness* and a couple of other movies by Tribe of Heart that dealt with compassion toward animals.

The discussions that we had about food, movies, and life in general were something that I had been missing for a long time. They filled a void within me.

During our third week together, we spent a couple of days going through my closets to purge all items of clothing that were made of silk, wool, leather, or fur. The problem with fur and leather was obvious; animals had to be killed for humans to use their skin. But I didn't understand what was wrong with silk, pearls, and wool.

Salaam explained that silk is made from the cocoons of silk worms, so the worms that are inside are killed. In the harvesting of pearls, the oysters are killed or at least injured. Although wool doesn't necessarily have to injure sheep, modern practices favor efficiency, which means that sheep are usually hurt. In a nutshell, whenever humans exploit animals for financial gain, the comfort of the animals is likely to be ignored, and the rights of the animals to lead natural, self-directed lives are denied.

Well, after going through my wardrobe, I wasn't left with much, but I was glad to rid myself of my hunting outfits. Salaam told me that there were a number of online businesses that sold belts and shoes made of leather alternatives and that I could also find "pleather" shoes and belts in mainstream stores, particularly lower-priced stores, if I looked hard enough. Anyway, a shopping spree to find new outfits made from cotton, rayon, and synthetics was something that I would enjoy.

By the end of the third week, my cravings for necromantic energy had subsided, and I was feeling satisfied eating vegan food.

"Let's celebrate," Salaam said. "And I know the perfect way. I've been invited to a fundraiser for the Vegetarian Society of the District of Columbia. It's going to be a semiformal reception at the US Botanical Gardens this Friday night. We can have dinner together first. What do you think? Is it a date?"

"You know, tomorrow is Friday. You're not giving me much time to plan," I teased, "but that doesn't matter. I'd love to go!"

The next day, I looked through what remained of my wardrobe and was fortunate to find that I still had a few evening dresses left. The one that I selected was midnight blue with a halter top that was sexy. However, the knee-length skirt flared away from the body, so overall, the dress wasn't too revealing. A sterling silver pendant necklace and silver colored sandals completed the outfit.

At precisely six o'clock, Salaam knocked on my door.

"Wow," he exclaimed. "You look lovely."

"And you look striking. I've never seen you in a suit and tie before! I'm impressed."

"Thank you. Do you have everything? Are you ready?"

"Yes."

"Okay. Let's go then."

We exited the front of the building and walked to Salaam's car, which was parked less than half a block away. This was my first time seeing what type of car he had chosen to purchase. Of course, it wasn't a luxury car. He was much too practical for that. But it was clean and shiny, and obviously, he took good care of it.

Salaam opened the passenger side door, helped me in, and gently closed the door behind me. Then he walked around the car and let himself in.

Once he had fastened his seatbelt and started the engine, he asked me, "Would you like to listen to some music?"

"Sure."

"Any particular type? I have all kinds here."

"Something soft. Classical maybe."

He immediately complied, and I had to wonder if he were always so solicitous or if he were making a special effort.

"I'm taking you to a restaurant that I think you'll really enjoy. It has delicious, healthful foods, and the chef takes presentation very seriously. You'll get a kick out of how beautifully the food is arranged on the plate. The chef is an artist, really."

When we arrived, I discovered that the "restaurant" was actually an old, renovated mansion that had been converted into a bed and breakfast. The restoration was remarkable. The intricate woodwork on the banisters and window trim appeared to have been recently stripped and refinished. On the olive green walls hung tapestries and tastefully framed landscape and still life paintings. The hardwood floors were covered with thick Oriental rugs. Traditional furnishings and Tiffany-style light fixtures matched the period of the architecture.

The *maître d'* led us to the dining room, which was larger than I expected it to be. Yet it was still cozy, with its burgundy walls, damask tablecloths, and candles on the five or so small tables. Each of the tables had formal place settings for two, from water goblet to coffee cup and from salad fork to dessert spoon.

In one corner of the room, an older gentleman wearing a black tuxedo played background music on an upright piano. He projected the ease of someone who had been playing for decades, simultaneously carrying on a conversation with a couple that was speaking to him softly. The only other couple in the room was dining at one of the tables, clearly enjoying themselves.

A pretty waitress in a black dress recited the menu to us from memory. It consisted of vegan appetizers, entrées, and desserts, including raw options. I selected a polenta dish, and Salaam selected a seaweed salad. Using neither pen nor paper, she took our orders. When she returned with our meals, both of them were, in fact, presented as elegantly as Salaam had said they would be. My triangular wedge of polenta was atop a layer of black beans arranged in a perfect circle surrounded by broccoli florets. The entire dish was drizzled with a sweet brown sauce.

"So how do you like it?"

"I've never been anywhere quite like this before. Both the restaurant and food are beautiful. I hope we'll come back so I can try some of the other entrées."

"I would love to bring you here again. This is how every meal should be enjoyed!"

We finished eating without much conversation, savoring the food, music, and each other's company. And although my meal was light, I felt satisfied.

"Would you like dessert?" the waitress asked.

Salaam looked at me, and I shook my head.

"No, thank you," he said.

"Very well. Enjoy the rest of the evening."

By the time that we left the restaurant, I was feeling more contented than I had in many years and was excited about going to the US Botanical Gardens. Despite having spent so much time in Washington, I had never visited this facility. In fact, I had passed the large greenhouse on Capitol Hill many times, but I never knew exactly what it was.

Two stylishly dressed women and a young man greeted us warmly at the main entrance.

"Hello, Salaam!"

"We're so glad you could make it!"

"How nice of you to come!"

Salaam hugged the two women and shook the man's hand. Then he introduced me as his "very dear friend." The three of them hugged me as well, and invited us to grab a drink and tour the spectacular indoor garden.

The gardens were incredibly beautiful at night. The Central Dome of the greenhouse rose 80 feet into the night sky and housed "The Jungle" – a collection of palm, banana, and other tropical trees, some of which almost touched the top of the glass enclosure. Closer to the ground were exotic plants, some with leaves as long as three or four feet, and others with a shower of tiny, delicate foliage.

Interspersed throughout the various shades of green, gray green, blue green, and brownish hues were flowers of every color, artfully displayed in a surprisingly natural-looking setting. Throughout each of the sections of the greenhouse, the overall lighting was dim, but spotlights and pendant lights showcased particular plants and groupings. On one side of the room, a foot bridge spanned a large pond for aquatic plants, and there were stairs that led to a walkway encircling the room three stories above ground so that visitors could get a closer view of the canopy of the trees.

Salaam and I climbed up to the second floor and stopped to admire a particularly distinctive tree.

"So, Miss Pearl, what do you want to be when you grow up?"

I smiled. "You know, I love music, and if I had a better voice, I would love to be a singer." I had never told anyone that before.

"Interesting! I always suspected that there was an artist inside of you, looking for a way to express herself."

"Realistically speaking, I'm not sure what I want to do now. I don't think I'll be satisfied exploiting the financial markets anymore. I want to do something meaningful, something that is creative or at least productive. Or helpful. I don't know what that is, though."

"You'll find your calling, or your calling will find you. Either way, I know you're going to do something great."

Salaam took my hand, and we went downstairs and continued our tour of the indoor garden. In addition to "The Jungle," there were several smaller rooms, each designed to support plants from different climates. Amidst the ferns in the "Garden Primeval," Salaam stopped walking and pulled me toward him.

He whispered in my ear, "I hope that you know that I really care about you."

That was exactly the wrong thing for him to say. I had been having a wonderful time, but my defenses sprang back up.

"I still don't understand why. You have no reason to care. I mean, about me in particular. I know why you want to reform me, but let's not mix the two things up."

"Not everything is about reason, logic. Sometimes, feelings just are what they are. Sometimes, your feelings are ahead of your intellect. There's something deep within you that my spirit recognizes and connects with."

He kissed me on the cheek, and we continued to stroll through the greenhouse in silence for another ten minutes or so. Then we said our goodbyes to the hosts and left. We engaged in very little conversation as we returned to my apartment.

Once we reached my door, Salaam said, "I hope you've been so quiet because you're thinking about what I said to you and not because

I've scared you off. I want many more evenings just as magical as the one that we just shared."

I said nothing as I opened my door. I didn't even look directly at him. Disappointed, he walked away. I was immediately tempted to call out to him, but instead, I went into my apartment and closed the door quietly behind me.

Chapter 16

The following day, I didn't get up until well after noon. The emotional confusion of the previous day had left me drained, yet I didn't sleep well. My apartment, my life, everything was being turned upside down, and Salaam's unpredictable behavior was adding to the turmoil. At times, it seemed that he truly wanted to include me in his life. At other times, it seemed that I was just another charity case or community service project. I was tired of trying to figure out what his intentions were. Anyway, it was time that I focused on what *I* needed and wanted.

When I got out of bed, the first thing that I noticed was the dress that I had worn the previous night, crumpled on the floor. I picked it up and put it in the hamper, deciding not to dwell on what had happened. Instead, I would challenge myself to finish reorganizing my home.

I took a quick bath and put on a pair of loose, comfortable jeans and a bright blue T-shirt before going downstairs to the kitchen to find something to eat. My refrigerator and pantry were now well stocked, but I didn't feel like cooking. I just put some cold cereal in a bowl and poured rice milk onto it. That would have to hold me until dinnertime.

Once I had finished eating, I called Salaam.

"Good morning, Pearl," he said in a sleepy voice.

"It's no longer morning. It's past one o'clock. Are you coming over today to help me finish?"

"Yeah. Sure. What time is it? Oh, yeah – you said one o'clock. Give me about an hour, hour and a half."

Salaam arrived a couple of hours later, looking a bit disheveled himself in a wrinkled red shirt and jeans. But however he may have been feeling, it was back to business right after we exchanged tense greetings. We both felt awkward.

Nevertheless, we tackled the challenge of veganizing my home. This was quite a task. We went through all of my toiletries and discarded anything that contained cholesterol, lanolin, beeswax, or other animal ingredients or that didn't include a statement that it hadn't been tested on animals. I was surprised that animal parts and secretions were in so many products. Salaam introduced me to Pangea's website so that I could order vegan replacement items.

Next, we began assessing my furniture. I had invested a lot of money in leather pieces, but fortunately, I had the resources to replace them all immediately.

For most of the afternoon, we only discussed whether a particular item should stay or go, so I was surprised when Salaam decided to try to engage me in conversation.

"So now that you're officially vegan, how do you think the rest of your life is going to change?"

"I don't really know yet. I haven't thought that far ahead. I do know that I want to find a new way to make a living, but I don't know what that will be. Becoming a lounge singer isn't exactly a realistic option for me!"

Salaam smiled but abruptly stopped and looked at his watch.

"Do you have to be somewhere?"

"Not really. I have some plans but not for another couple of hours. I almost forgot..."

"It's okay for you to leave now if you would like to. I wouldn't hold it against you."

"No, no. It's really fine. Let's continue – but we'd better call someone now to make arrangements to have your stuff picked up."

I called the Salvation Army and scheduled a time for them to take away my furniture and clothing the next business day. Meanwhile, Salaam prepared a simple dinner of rice, beans, and sautéed kale and tomatoes for us.

Working well into the night, we moved everything that would be leaving my apartment into the living room near the top of the stairs.

"I'm exhausted," I finally said. "Can we take a break?"

"Yeah, I'm worn out, too. Let's lie down on your bed for a while."

My bedroom, which I had always kept so perfectly arranged, was now completely disorganized. The Persian rug, which was made of wool, was rolled up and waiting for the movers in the living room. My headboard was covered in leather, so it had to go, too. My lamps were adorned with genuine pearls, so they were on their way out. Even my silk sheets had been removed, washed, and packed up. My pillows were filled with down, so we put them in large bags, unsure whether the charity would take them or we would have to throw them away.

Fortunately, I had a set of cotton sheets and a cotton blanket that I was able to use to make up the bed. I did so quickly while Salaam moved a few things out of the way.

"You should get into bed first," I said, "because my lamps are downstairs. I don't want you to trip over anything after I turn off the overhead light."

He nodded and undressed, absentmindedly dropping his shirt and jeans where he stood. I watched him, admiring his body clothed only in his briefs again, but this time also feeling a deep appreciation for his generous spirit. I very much wanted him, but I didn't expect to have him. We didn't seem to be able to connect.

Once he got under the covers, I turned off the light and carefully made my way over to the bed. Not wanting to face rejection from him again, I took off my jeans and slid out of my bra but put my T-shirt back on before getting into bed.

He was lying on his back, and despite my reservations, I stretched out beside him, with my hand resting on his chest and my head resting on his upper arm.

"Thank you for everything," I whispered.

He lifted his head and kissed me gently on the forehead. I responded by kissing him lightly on the lips. Kissing him evoked a deep sensation of closeness. I hadn't kissed anyone in ages, and in the past, it hadn't been to express love. This was new.

I would have been content to simply lie next to him all night, but as I moved away to end the kiss, he pulled me back toward him. He pressed his lips against mine, and then he tugged at my lower lip with his lips. He gently outlined the shape of my mouth with his tongue, before entering my mouth and exploring my tongue with his. As I responded in kind, his heart rate quickened and his breathing was audible.

"From the moment that we first spoke in the lobby," he said softly, "I knew what you were and what you could be. You're just beginning to turn your life around, but I already know you're going to do something incredible. I want to be with you when that happens, and I want to be with you now. We know each other's secrets. We know where we've been and who we are. I've been waiting for us to really know each other so that when I share myself with you, it won't just be physical. It will be complete. I want to give you all of me. I hope you will accept me."

I said nothing.

His hands searched for my skin through the tangle of fabric which was my shirt and the sheets. I let him.

"Take this off," he said, and I sat up to comply.

He pushed the covers to the foot of the bed and kneeled in front of me, helping me to remove my top. He kissed my mouth again while we were kneeling there, encircling me in his arms. Supporting my weight in one arm, he pressed me backwards, planting kisses down my neck and all over my breasts. It was as though he was hungry and wanted to devour me.

Somehow, he sustained the connection that we had through our kiss as he removed our remaining clothes and lowered me onto the bed.

"Wait," I finally managed to utter. The word barely escaped from my lips, more a warning to myself than a command to Salaam.

"Please don't make me," he pleaded between kisses. "Don't you want me?"

"Yes."

I gave in to my desires, and we were one. We moved together to a rhythm outside of ourselves. My muscles tensed and then fluttered. Simultaneously, we released ourselves to each another.

"I love you," he whispered. "You are so beautiful."

Tears filled my eyes. In that instant, I knew that Salaam was right. I *was* beautiful, and I was no longer a vampire. I drifted off into a restful sleep.

I awoke very early the next morning, before the sun had even risen. Not wanting to disturb Salaam, I gently extricated myself from his sleepy embrace and got out of bed. I knew deep within me that I had really changed. My spirit felt entirely different, light and free. I put on a sweater and my favorite pair of jeans and went into the bathroom to wash my face.

My mirror was still hidden by the valance, but I wanted to see myself. I climbed onto the vanity and removed the heavy fabric that had hung there for so long. When I uncovered the mirror, I was able to face myself.

Gazing into my own eyes, I realized what I had to do. I retrieved a box of stationery and a pen from my office and went onto the balcony. Under the glow of the street light, I composed a letter to Salaam.

My dearest Salaam,

I want to thank you for everything that you've done for me. When I met you, I was selfish, cruel, and thoughtless. My sole purpose in living was to indulge in self gratification. I didn't care about or respect anyone else. I didn't recognize that others have the same right as I do to live out their natural lifespans and to live the full range of experiences that the Creator intended for them. Now I understand that I'm not greater than anyone else; each life is unique and has equal intrinsic value. I'm not in this life alone; we're all interconnected. You taught me this.

I love you, and you're a part of me now. But I have to move on. I've interrupted your life for too long, and I've disrupted your relationship with Udah. If she's the right woman for you, I'll be happy to know that you two are able to work things out and get together.

I never appreciated the value of your friends. I've been rude to Lynford and especially vicious to Udah. Please express my contrition to them. I hope that they can forgive me.

I've done a lot of damage that can't be undone. As you like to say, the past can't be changed. But I can try to get a fresh start in a new place. I'll figure out a way to do some good in this world, hopefully enough good to outweigh the bad.

You opened your heart to me. You saw things in me that I didn't even know were there. You helped me see myself as I should be. Because of you, I am no longer a monster to be feared and despised by God's other children. I am the human being that I was meant to be.

I will love you forever.

Pearl

Once I signed the letter, I looked up to discover that the sun had risen. It was a clear and beautiful day, and for the first time in decades, I was going to be able to enjoy it.

I moved into the light, and it did not burn. I was actually experiencing sunlight on my skin! I was finally free. I was human again. I was overjoyed and filled with optimism.

I placed the letter in an envelope and put it on the bed next to Salaam. Then I packed a few things in a small bag and left the apartment for the last time.

Epilogue

I closed the door behind me and left Salaam asleep in my bed. It was a bittersweet moment. I would surely miss him, but I needed to make the rest of my journey on my own.

As I walked into the lobby, for the first time during the day, I saw that it was filled with beautiful sunlight. I was brimming with anticipation for what I would find as I stepped into a new world.

Suddenly, my thoughts were interrupted by a shrill voice calling out my name.

"Pearl!"

Udah was stepping out of the elevator in a rage. I almost didn't recognize her. Her hair was pulled back; her face was made up; and she was wearing a black evening gown and high heels. Clearly, this was all intended for a special night that had never happened because of me.

"Udah, I'm glad to see you. This gives me a chance to tell you –"

"I already know. I've been trying to reach Salaam all night, and he's not in his apartment. He must have been with you."

"Yes, but –"

"You won't get away with this. It's time to lay my cards on the table, to talk plainly. I know that you're a demon and that he once was, too. I was the one that helped him reclaim his soul, and I'm not going to let you drag him back into hell with you."

"But you don't understand! Stop talking for a minute, and listen to me."

Udah had a look on her face that I'd never seen before, wild and furious. Her eyes were shining. Sweat glistened on her brow, and her limbs were trembling.

"Silence! You *shall* respect me!"

Her words sent a chill through me. This woman, whom I once dismissed as a minor annoyance, now frightened me. I backed away from her, moving slowly toward the door, but she continued to approach me, matching my movements step for step.

Pointing at me, she cried, "Don't you dare move another muscle! I have no more patience for you. Even *my* compassion has its limits."

My mind told my body to flee, but I was rooted in place, held still by an unseen force. Helpless and terrified, I understood how my prey had felt when I immobilized them.

Then, by some act of providence, Salaam came running into the lobby, his bare chest heaving up and down.

"Udah!" he gasped. "What are you doing?"

She turned to look at him, but continued pointing at me, holding me in her unnatural grip. Salaam stopped several feet away from her.

"What are *you* doing here?" Udah asked.

"Your anger is so great that it woke me! I could've heard your words a mile away even if you had been whispering!"

"Have you come to rescue her? If so, it's too late."

"Udah, don't do this. She really has changed. Please let her go!"

"No. It's over for your precious Pearl."

"Please," Salaam begged. "We're on the same side."

Udah glared at him. "Not anymore."

She turned back toward me and extended both of her hands out in my direction. Gazing upward as if in a trance, she began to speak.

"Papa Niser, hear me! It is I, your great great grandchild, Udah –"

"Silence!" Salaam commanded. His tone was familiar. I had used it many times on my prey, but I had never expected to hear it coming from him.

Udah's hands dropped to her sides, and she bowed her head – but only for the briefest moment. Almost immediately, she turned to Salaam, struck out at him, and without even touching him, threw him against the wall.

Still paralyzed where I stood, I could only watch and tremble.

As Salaam lay crumpled on the floor, Udah began her incantation again, arms and face raised. This time, she completed her recitation.

"Papa Niser, hear me! It is I, your great great grandchild, Udah. Your blood runs through my veins. My will is your will. Do my bidding. Send this foul thing away. Let her reap what she has sown. She has rejoiced in the suffering of others. Turn the tables. She has killed without mercy. Cast her into a place and time that befits her. Do it now!"

Two thin rays of energy descended from above, entered Udah's eyes, and exited her fingertips. The energy streams merged into one and hit me as a powerful force to the center of my body. The blast pushed me backwards and out of the glass doors that led to the street. I continued to travel backwards and upwards at an incredible speed. My belly was on fire, but my skin was ice cold. My ears were assailed by a deafening roar. Before me, I could see buildings, then streets, the city, continent, planet, blinding lights and bright colors. The journey seemed to last an eternity, but finally, thankfully, it ended as I was thrown to the ground.

I raised my face to try to see where I was. There were dozens of sullen, emaciated people dressed in rags. Some were moaning, some were suffering in silence. Before I could look around, a painful blow connected with the back of my head. Everything became darkness and silence.

Resources

Compassion Over Killing (COK)
http://www.cok.net/

Farm Animal Rights Movement (FARM)
http://www.farmusa.org/about.htm

Michael Greger, M.D.
http://www.drgreger.org/

Humane Society of the United States
http://www.humanesociety.org/

People for the Ethical Treatment of Animals (PETA)
http://www.peta.org

Physicians Committee for Responsible Medicine (PCRM)
http://www.pcrm.org/

Poplar Spring Animal Sanctuary
http://animalsanctuary.org/

United Poultry Concerns
http://www.upc-online.org/

Vegan Society
http://www.vegansociety.com/

Vegetarian Resource Group
http://www.vrg.org/

Vegetarian Society of DC (VSDC)
http://www.vsdc.org/

Vegetarian Union of North America (VUNA)
http://www.ivu.org/vuna/

About the Author

Merlene Alicia Vassall has been an avid reader and writer since childhood and has been fascinated with vampires for just as long. Her ideas about the vampire mythology have been influenced over the years by the campy Dracula movies of the '70s to the more recent interpretations. In contrast, Merlene has been vegetarian since the mid 1980s and vegan since 1996, primarily for reasons of compassion toward animals. *The Vampire and The Vegan, Book I: Food* ties together these two diverse interests.

Professionally, Merlene has worked with nonprofit organizations since 1983, first as an employee and then via her firm, Technical Assistance & Support Consultants. For more than two decades, her services have been utilized by a range of progressive nonprofit organizations to raise funds to meet the needs of at-risk children, disadvantaged communities, and developing nations.

She has been actively involved with the Vegetarian Society of the District of Columbia (VSDC) since 1996. She has served on the VSDC Board of Directors and raised approximately $150,000 for the VSDC Eat Smart Program, which she conceptualized. Since the program began in 2004, hundreds of individuals have learned how to make the transition to a healthful vegan diet.

Merlene earned her Bachelor of Science from Cornell University's College of Human Ecology and her Juris Doctor from Georgetown University Law Center.

The Vampire and The Vegan, Book I: Food is Merlene's first novel. Her next book will be the sequel, *The Vampire and The Vegan, Book II: Livestock.*

CPSIA information can be obtained
at www.ICGtesting.com
Printed in the USA
FFOW02n0513290515
13706FF